"What if I say [...]
Would you believe [...]

"I would pray fervently that is true," Emma replied.

"Not exactly what I wanted to hear."

She crossed her arms tightly over her chest. "It's the best I can do."

"Then maybe I should tell your father I've changed my mind." He pulled back. A shadow slipped across his eyes.

Was it pain? Had she hurt him? That was never her intention. "I'm sorry."

"Don't be. It's best to get our feelings out in the open. I'll speak to your father tomorrow."

"But you understand machines. You will know what can be fixed and what is junk fit only for scrap. At least he'll make a little money off that."

"And making money is important, isn't it? Of course it is. What woman wants to go into a marriage empty-handed?"

She drew back in shock. "Marriage? Who said anything about marriage?"

After thirty-five years as a nurse, **Patricia Davids** hung up her stethoscope to become a full-time writer. She enjoys spending her free time visiting her grandchildren, doing some long-overdue yard work and traveling to research her story locations. She resides in Wichita, Kansas. Pat always enjoys hearing from her readers. You can visit her online at patriciadavids.com.

Books by Patricia Davids

Love Inspired

The Amish Bachelors

An Amish Harvest
An Amish Noel

Lancaster Courtships

The Amish Midwife

Brides of Amish Country

The Christmas Quilt
A Home for Hannah
A Hope Springs Christmas
Plain Admirer
Amish Christmas Joy
The Shepherd's Bride
The Amish Nanny
An Amish Family Christmas: A Plain Holiday
An Amish Christmas Journey
Amish Redemption

Visit the Author Profile page at Harlequin.com for more titles.

An Amish Noel

Patricia Davids

HARLEQUIN® LOVE INSPIRED®

Recycling programs
for this product may
not exist in your area.

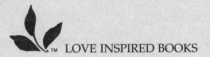

™ LOVE INSPIRED BOOKS

ISBN-13: 978-0-373-81877-8

An Amish Noel

Copyright © 2015 by Patricia MacDonald

www.Harlequin.com

Printed in U.S.A.

If thou, Lord, shouldest mark iniquities, O Lord,
who shall stand?
But there is forgiveness with thee,
that thou mayest be feared.
I wait for the Lord, my soul doth wait,
and in His word do I hope.
—*Psalms* 130:3–5

This book is dedicated with Love and Hugs
to my granddaughter Shantel.
Merry Christmas, honey.
PS: Don't forget to do your chores.

Chapter One

"He's not going to try and cross the river. No one is that stupid." Luke Bowman drew back on the reins of the draft horses pulling the large bobsled. The massive gray Percherons stopped, but they tossed their shaggy heads, making the harness bells jingle. They were eager to finish the task and head home. Their snorts sent duel puffs of white mist into the cold November air. Luke watched in disbelief as a snowmobile with two riders continued to barrel toward the frozen river winding through the snow-covered valley below his father's cornfield.

Noah, Luke's youngest brother, leaned on his ax handle as he stood behind the driver's seat. "I remember when you did it on Jim Morgan's snowmobile. More than once. That looks like the same machine."

It did look like the same machine, but Luke doubted it was his *Englisch* friend aboard. More than likely it was Jim's younger brother Brian riding into trouble. "We never crossed this early in the year. The ice isn't thick enough. It won't hold them."

Noah pulled his scarf up to cover his face. "This cold snap has been bitter even for late November. Maybe the ice is thicker than you think."

Luke didn't mind the cold. His stint in prison made him cherish every moment he could spend out in the open. "It would have to be this cold a lot longer to freeze running water."

He and Noah had come out to gather a load of firewood from the stand of trees along the river. Four inches of fresh snow from the night before made easy pulling for the team. The sled was three-quarters full of logs lashed together, and the men were on their way home.

Luke watched the snowmobilers a second longer, then he turned the horses toward the river. Noah almost lost his balance on the flat sled at the unexpected move and had to grab hold of the seatback to keep from falling off. "What are you doing?"

"We're gonna pull those fools out of the water unless they drown before we reach them."

The red-and-white machine didn't stop. It hit the river's edge at a fast clip and traveled a full fifty feet out onto the ice before the front end broke through, spilling the riders. Luke shouted at the team and slapped the reins, sending the horses into a fast trot across the snow-covered field, knowing he might be too late. If the riders were dragged under the icc by the current, they would drown.

One of the snowmobile riders had been thrown clear of the open water. He lay sprawled face-down on the ice. The second rider was desperately trying to claw his way out of the river but the edge of the icc kept breaking in front of him. The snowmobile teetered precariously, half in and half out of the water as it hung by the rear tread.

"Whoa, fellas." Luke drew the horses to a stop at the riverbank. He saw the first rider trying to stand. It was a young boy.

"Help! Somebody help us!"

Luke shouted to the boy struggling to get to the other rider. "Lie down! Spread your weight out on the ice!"

Tossing the lines to Noah, Luke jumped off the sled. From the toolbox under the seat, he grabbed his ax along with a coil of rope and started toward the river.

The boy was following Luke's orders. He lay down and wiggled toward the rider in the water. He grasped his buddy, but Luke saw he was too small to pull the bigger boy to safety.

Luke quickly tied a loop around his waist as

Noah joined him at the river's edge. "I should go. I'm smaller."

Luke considered it for a second then shook his head. "I'd rather drown than face *Mamm* and tell her I let you get killed. Take a hitch around that tree so you can pull me back if I go through. The current is strong in this curve."

"Don't make *me* tell *Mamm* I let *you* drown."

"I'll do my best. Hang on, boys, I'm coming!" Luke hacked a long branch from a nearby tree and stepped out on the ice. The thick layer of fresh snow made it hard to see where he was putting his feet. He used the branch to feel his way, making sure the ice was solid until he got near the two boys. At that point, he lay down and edged toward them. The cold bit through his pants and gloves as he crab-scuttled along.

"Hurry!" the little one shouted, looking over his shoulder.

Luke recognized him. "Alvin Swartzentruber, are you okay?"

"Help me, Luke." The fourteen-year-old stayed sprawled on the ice, holding on to the other rider.

Every time Luke thought he could move faster, the ice cracked with a sickening sound beneath him. Would it hold? He couldn't help the boys if he went through, too. Finally, he worked his way to within a few feet of them and stopped, not wanting to add his weight to their precarious spot. "I thought you had better sense than this, Alvin."

"I reckon I didn't today."

"I reckon not. Who you got with you?"

"It's Roy. Hurry, Luke, I can't hold him."

"You can. I'm almost there. Roy, can you hear me?" Roy was Alvin's older brother. Luke knew them well. He knew their sister, Emma, even better, or he had once. They didn't speak to each other these days.

"Help." Roy's voice was barely audible through his chattering teeth. His lips were tinged with blue and his eyes were wild with fear.

Luke was close enough to reach them with the branch. He slid the end past Alvin. "Hang on to this, Roy, and let go of your brother."

He was afraid the bigger boy would pull the smaller one in if he went under.

Roy grasped the limb with first one hand and then the other. "I—I got it."

Luke needed room to pull Roy free. "Alvin, roll away from the hole and go to my brother. Stay on your hands and knees until you get close to the shore. Follow my trail. The ice was strong enough to hold me—it should hold you."

With the younger boy headed to safety, Luke inched closer to Roy. He heard the ice beneath him groan.

I'm not ready to meet you, Lord, but if this is the reason You got me out of prison and put me

here today, at least help me save this boy first.
Don't give Emma one more reason to hate me.

He forced his thoughts away from Emma and the heartache he had caused her. "Roy, I'm gonna slip a loop of rope over you. You're gonna have to get it under your arms. Can you do that?"

"I think so."

"Goot." Luke worked the rope off over his head and shoulders and prepared to lay the loop over Roy.

"Is…Alvin…safe?"

Luke glanced back. The boy was climbing the bank to where Noah stood with the rope snubbed around a tree. "He's fine. You will be, too, in a minute."

"I can't…hold on. Can't…feel…my hands." Roy started to sink.

"Don't give up."

The boy's head went under. Luke made a grab for him, plunging his hands into the frigid water.

Emma looked up in relief when she heard a horse and buggy come into the yard. Rising from her quilting frame, she crossed to the window. Her father should've been back an hour ago. She was anxious to hear what his doctor had told him about the fatigue he couldn't shake.

Her father, Zachariah Swartzentruber, had always been a big man. He stood six feet tall, but she hadn't noticed until this moment how his clothes seemed to hang on his frame now or how bent he was becoming. He moved slowly, as if his actions were painful or difficult as he got out of the buggy. She hoped the English doctor had discovered what was wrong and prescribed some medicine to make her father better.

She held open the door as he came up the walk. "How was your trip, *Daed*?"

"It was a long way. The traffic gets worse every time I must go into town. The foolish *Englisch* rush past without a care in their big cars."

Their little Amish community of Bowmans Crossing was more than five miles off the state highway. Even so, the traffic in the area was increasing, as were the accidents involving buggies and cars.

She waited until her father took a seat at the kitchen table. "What did the doctor have to say?"

"Is there any *kaffi*?"

"*Ja*, I made a pot about an hour ago." Going to the stove, she pulled a brown mug from the shelf overhead and filled it to the brim with the strong brew from her coffeepot.

"*Danki.*" He accepted the cup from her hand and stirred in a heaping spoonful of sugar. He sat staring into the liquid, stirring slowly.

Fear crept into Emma's heart. It wasn't like her father to be so quiet. Something was wrong. "What did the doctor have to say, *Daed*?"

Her father took a sip of coffee. "This is *goot*.

You always could make good *kaffi*. Not like your mother. Her *kaffi* was always weak as dishwater."

Emma swallowed hard. It was unusual for her father to speak about his deceased wife. The Amish rarely talked about loved ones who had passed on. Her worry spiked, but she knew better than to keep pressing him. When he was ready, he would tell her what the doctor had discovered.

She poured herself a cup and carried it to the table. "*Mamm* was a frugal woman. She could stretch a nickel into a dime and give you two cents change."

A tiny smiled lifted the corner of his lip. "That she could. I think sometimes she used the same grounds for three days in a row."

"I like my coffee stout. I would rather save on other things."

He looked at her then. "You need a new dress. I would not have you looking so shabby."

The front of her everyday dress was stained and the cuffs were getting thin, but it had at least another year of use before it went into the rag bag. "I can't wear a good dress to do laundry and scrub floors. This one will do for a little longer. My other workday dress is not so worn, and I have a nice Sunday dress. I don't need anything else."

"If a fella was to come courting, you'd want to look nice. We can afford the material."

They couldn't, but that wasn't the point. She

saw her father had something serious on his mind. "No one is coming to court me. What's wrong, *Daed*?"

"Wayne Hochstetler intends to ask you out."

She sat back in surprise. "Wayne? How do you know this?"

Wayne was a widower and the eldest son of their neighbor to the west. He and his family belonged to a different church group, one that was more conservative, but Wayne was known as a stalwart member of the Amish faith and a good farmer. His father was the bishop of their church district.

"I spoke with his father. Wayne is looking for a wife. He has a young daughter who needs a mother."

"I hope he finds one, but what makes you think I would be interested in going out with him?"

"Because it's time you married. It's past time. You will be thirty soon. That is old enough to be settled."

"I'm barely twenty-five, *Daed*."

"That is still plenty old enough. I want you to seriously consider Wayne as a husband. His father and I are good friends. This would make us happy."

"I thought marriage was a question of who would make *me* happy." She once believed Luke Bowman was that man, but she had been mistaken. Sadly mistaken.

"Love can grow from friendship and mutual respect. If there is someone else, *dochder*, please tell me now."

"I have enough to do taking care of you and the boys. There isn't anyone I'm interested in."

"*Goot*, then you will consider Wayne?"

"Not until you give me a better reason than my age and your friendship with his father. What's this about? Why this sudden interest in seeing me married off? I have plenty of time to meet the right man and fall in love."

He sighed heavily. "You may have the time, but I do not. The news from the doctor was not *goot*, but it was what I have been expecting."

Her heart pounded painfully, stealing her breath. "You are frightening me. What did he say?"

"I have inherited the same disease that took my father when you were but a small child. My kidneys are failing. The doctor thinks I have a year, maybe two, before it is my time to stand before God and be judged."

She stared at him in disbelief. "Is the doctor sure? Can't there be some mistake? I know you've been ill, but you'll get better. You can see another doctor."

He reached across the table and took her hand in his. "I knew this was coming when I started having the same type of pain that wore down my father. I can only pray that God has chosen to spare my sons."

"And me? Can this disease come to me and my children?"

"You forget. You are my stepdaughter. I married your mother when you were only a babe. Your father died in a farming accident. This disease I inherited cannot come to you."

It was true. She always forgot that Zachariah wasn't her real father. "You have been a father to me in every sense of the word save that one small thing. I could not love you more if we were bound by blood."

"You are a true child of my heart, Emma, but I won't be able to care for you and the boys for much longer. I need to know someone will look after the lot of you when I'm gone. It falls to you now. The boys are too young."

"I don't have to be married to take care of my brothers. You know I will always do that. The church will help us."

"Wayne has a prosperous farm. Combined with my land, it will be more than enough. You will not be dependent on the charity of others. Do not mistake me—there's nothing wrong with accepting charity when you need it, but it is much better not to need it. I'm not afraid to face death but I am afraid of leaving you and your brothers without a secure future. Can you understand that?"

"*Ja*, I do. I can't believe this is happening." She didn't want to believe it. Not her big strong father. There had to be some mistake.

"I'm sorry to burden you with this news, but in one sense, it is a blessing. Few men are given the chance to know when their end is coming. I have time to prepare. You will have time to prepare as well. You must find someone to care for you when I cannot. Wayne is a *goot* man. A fine farmer. I hope you will consider him."

Emma arose and carried her mug to the kitchen sink. Setting it carefully on the counter, she stared out the window. How could she refuse Zachariah's request? She couldn't. Everything she had, everything she believed in, was due to the kindness and love of the man who had chosen to become her father.

"Where are the boys?" he asked.

She stared out the kitchen window at the snow-covered farm looking pristine and sparkling as the clouds parted and sunshine chased away the gloomy afternoon. God's beautiful white blanket covered the holes in the barn roof and disguised the junk her father piled up along the sides of the sheds. No one could see how the henhouse roof sagged or how badly it needed to be replaced. "They took a load of firewood to Jim Morgan's place. They should have been back by now."

"You know how they like to look at Jim's toys.

Maybe he is giving them a ride on his motorcycle again."

"I hope not." She hated that her brothers were fascinated with *Englisch* vehicles. She disliked that Jim and his brother encouraged them, but her family needed the money Jim was willing to pay for the wood the boys cut and hauled.

Her poor brothers. They would be heartbroken when they learned this news about their father. She wanted to ease the pain for them, but she didn't know how. Tears pricked the back of her eyes. She brushed them away. "I wish they would come home. I know you want to share this news with them, sad though it is."

"I will tell them, but not yet. Not today."

She turned to face him. "Why wait?"

He stirred his coffee without looking at her. "Christmas is coming. You know how excited Alvin is about his school Christmas program. I don't want to ruin that for him. This news can wait until after the New Year. A month or two won't make any difference. Perhaps by then they will have the news of your coming marriage to cheer them up and make them feel secure."

"I see your point." Except that meant she would have to carry the burden of this information alone.

"I hear someone coming. Is it the boys?"

The sound of hoofbeats reached her. She glanced out the window and her traitorous heart gave the same funny little flip it always did when she caught sight of Luke Bowman. He drew his buggy to a stop in front of the house.

Luke. The man she had once hoped to marry. The same man who had made it painfully clear that he didn't care about her at all. The memory of their parting years ago still had the power to bring tears to her eyes.

Jim Morgan had been the one who told her Luke was leaving that night. She had packed a bag and rushed to find him before it was too late. At the bus station, she had gripped his arm, willing him to see how much she cared.

"I love you, Luke. More than my own life. More than my family. I'll go anywhere as long as I can be with you. You need me as much as I need you. I know you love me."

He brushed her hand aside. His face was blank as he stared at the ground. "You don't get it, Emma. I don't need you. I don't want you tagging after me. Stay here. Live a simple life. Be happy with some farmer and have six kids of your own."

"I don't want to stay without you. I love you. Please, let me come with you."

"Why would I? You've become a nuisance. I don't love you, Emma. I never did." He turned away and started to board the bus as her heart broke into tiny pieces. On the steps, he paused. "Forget about me. Find someone else."

He took a seat by the window and left her

weeping at the bus station. He never looked back. She knew because she had watched until the bus was gone from sight.

She had meant nothing to him, while he had meant everything to her.

But not anymore.

It was a blessing that he had rejected her offer to go out into the world with him. Nineteen, lovestruck and foolishly naive, she hadn't understood the powerful hold his growing drug use had on him then. She thought her prayers and her love could change him, save him from himself, but she had been wrong. Luke had been caught in a downward spiral that brought shame and heartache to her and to his family. He had disappeared into the city where he went from using drugs to selling them until he was arrested. It had taken time in prison to free him from his addiction.

Emma blew out a deep breath as she watched Luke get out of his buggy. She'd gotten over her feelings for him ages ago. Now, he was simply someone she chose to avoid. In the year and a half that he had been back among the Amish, she'd managed never to be alone with him.

Pushing her painful memories and broken dreams into the deep recesses of her heart, she dumped her coffee down the drain. "Luke Bowman is here."

"Luke? I wonder what he wants."

Chapter Two

"Are you going to come in with me?" Still seated in Luke's buggy, young Alvin gazed fearfully at the house.

"*Ja*, I'll come in." Luke knew exactly how the boy felt. He'd been in the same position more than once in his life—having to face the consequence of his foolhardincss. Thc boy had learned a hard lesson today. Older brothers did not always know best.

Luke stood in the cold air waiting for the boy to get out. His hands still ached, but at least he had the feeling back in them now. His buggy horse whinnied to Zachariah's horse hitched at the rail in front of the house. The black gelding nickered back. Flecks of foam on the animal proved the horse had covered more than a few miles recently. Why hadn't he been put away? It was bad for a sweaty horse to be left standing in the cold. Zachariah knew that. Maybe he was leaving again soon.

"She's gonna be mad." Alvin scooted a shade closer to the open door but didn't get out.

Luke knew whom the boy meant. "She'll be thankful that you're safe. Trust me."

"For a little bit. Then she's gonna be mad. You don't know what my *shveshtah* is like when she gets her feathers ruffled."

"Actually, I do know what your sister is like when she's angry."

Luke didn't bother trying to explain ancient history to the worried boy with him, but he still recalled the tongue lashings Emma had given him when she'd discovered he and Jim were experimenting with drugs. His life would have been a lot better if he'd taken her scolding to heart, but he hadn't. He'd let the drugs pull him deeper and deeper into trouble until he ended up in prison. Like most fools, he'd had to learn his lesson the hard way. Even now, he worried that he might fall back into his old ways without the threat of prison hanging over his head.

Alvin finally got out of the buggy. Luke followed him up the porch steps. At the door, Alvin drew a deep breath and turned the doorknob. Luke followed him in. Emma and Zachariah were waiting for them in the clean and cheery kitchen. The room had wide-plank pine floors. A blue checkered cloth covered the long table in the center of the room. A star quilt in bright shades of red and white covered a quilting frame in front of the far window. The mouthwatering smell of roasting meat and vegetables came from the oven. A pan of rolls sat rising on the stovetop. Emma had always been a good cook.

Luke took his black hat off. Alvin pulled his off, too, and stood at Luke's side, staring at the floor. From his own experiences, Luke knew Alvin wouldn't be able to sink through it and disappear no matter how hard he wished he could. He put a hand on the boy's shoulder and nodded to Alvin's family. "Afternoon, Emma, Zachariah."

"*Goot* to see you, Luke. What brings you here with my youngest in tow? Has he been up to some mischief?"

"Alvin, where is Roy?" Emma didn't bother to acknowledge Luke. He was used to it, but it still hurt when she pointedly ignored him.

"There was a sort of accident," Alvin muttered.

"What kind of accident?" Zachariah rose unsteadily to his feet. Emma stood beside him wide-eyed. She pressed a hand to her chest.

"Roy is okay," Luke added quickly to reassure them. He pushed Alvin forward. "You had best tell them everything from the beginning."

Alvin nodded, took a deep breath and looked at his sister. "We took the wood to Jim Morgan's house like you told us to do, Emma. We unloaded it and stacked it in his shed. When we were done, Jim let us sit on his snowmobile. The red-and-white one that goes so fast. You've seen it, haven't you?"

"And?" Emma prompted, the concern in her eyes giving way to speculation.

"Jim went inside to get our money, and his brother Brian showed Roy how to start the snowmobile. Brian let us take it for a little ride. Just a short one. We were coming right back. It was loads of fun. Then…"

Her eyes narrowed to slits. She propped her hands on her hips. "Then what?"

"Roy drove it out on the river," Luke continued when it was clear that Alvin was out of courage. "The machine broke through the ice. Alvin was thrown clear, but Roy was dumped in the water. Fortunately, Noah and I saw the whole thing. We fished Roy out and got him back to my folks' place. *Mamm* and Rebecca thought it best that he stay in bed for a day or so to make sure he recovers and doesn't come down with pneumonia."

Rebecca was married to Luke's oldest brother. She was Emma's cousin and had worked as a lay nurse in the community before she married Samuel. Luke knew Emma would trust her judgment over anyone else on the subject of her brother's health.

Zachariah sat down. "Sounds like my boy took more than a little dunking."

Luke turned his hat in his hands. "He was in the water for a good bit."

"He got swept under the ice, but Luke saved him," Alvin said, looking up with admiration in his eyes.

Uncomfortable with the praise, Luke ruffled the boy's blond hair. "God helped a little. He kept me from falling through the ice, too."

"I know how treacherous the river ice is this time of year. You risked your life to save my son. *Danki.*" Zachariah rose to his feet again and held his hand out.

Luke accepted the man's thanks and shook his hand. "Anyone would have done the same."

Emma rubbed a hand across her forehead. "So Roy has ruined a machine that costs hundreds if not thousands of dollars. How are we going to pay for it? Does your brother possess a single grain of common sense? What came over him to try and ride a snowmobile? And you just went along with him as if it were okay. I honestly don't know what to do with you, Alvin."

"Told you," the boy whispered under his breath. He stared at the floor again.

Luke was hard-pressed not to smile. "I managed to get a rope on the snowmobile and pull it off the river after Roy was safe. It will take some work, but it will run again."

"You went back out on the ice? You risked your life to retrieve a stupid machine? What is wrong with you, Luke Bowman?" Emma's eyes snapped with fury.

Taken aback by her anger, he gaped at her. She had no idea how attractive she was with her cheeks flushed with color and her hands propped on her shapely hips. Her dress was a deep blue, the same shade as her eyes, and her white *kapp* accented the fiery red of her hair. She was a fine figure of a woman now. Not at all like the skinny girl that he'd dated back when he was nineteen. They had both changed, but he remembered the sweet taste of her lips as if it were yesterday.

"What were you thinking?" Emma demanded.

Luke fastened his gaze on the floor. Best not to think about the times he had kissed those pert lips. "I was thinking it would be a shame to let a fine machine fall into a watery grave. Jim is a good friend of mine."

"You are unbelievable!" Emma stormed out of the room and up the stairs. The sound of a door slamming overhead reverberated through the house.

Zachariah swung his gaze to Luke. "Forgive Emma's temper. She has had a trying day."

"Having Emma mad at me is nothing new. I'll live." Luke quelled his desire to follow her and make amends. It wouldn't do any good, anyway.

She could barely stay in the same room with him, let alone listen to his apology.

Zachariah laid a hand on Alvin's shoulder. "I'm glad you are safe. I give God thanks for His mercy. Are you well enough to go take care of my horse?"

"Sure."

"Danki, sohn."

When the boy left the room, Zachariah gestured toward the chairs at the table. "Please, sit down, Luke."

"I didn't plan to stay."

"Humor an old man. Sit for a spell."

"You're not so old, Zachariah." Against his better judgment, Luke took a seat. He knew having him around made Emma uncomfortable. If he heard her coming downstairs, he'd leave.

Zachariah leaned back in his chair. "I feel as if I am a hundred today. How is your family?"

"Everyone is fine. I don't know if Emma told you, but Samuel and Rebecca are expecting a child in May." Luke's oldest brother had married Zachariah's niece a year ago. Rebecca and Emma had remained close friends.

"She mentioned it the other day. That is *goot*. A blessing to be sure. Is your father's business keeping all your brothers busy?"

Luke's father owned a woodworking shop. Luke and his four brothers as well as several other carpenters from the area made furniture for a high-end furniture dealer in Cincinnati. "We've been busy, but *Daed* plans to close for a month after Christmas and take *Mamm* down to Pinecrest, Florida, for a few weeks. They haven't had a vacation in years. *Mamm* says she can't take the cold the way she used to. She wants to visit the Amish settlement by the sea."

"I understand how she feels. I have often wanted to go there myself. Luke, I wanted to talk to you because you're a fellow who knows his way around machinery. I've collected a fair number of items that need some restoration work before they can be resold."

Luke smiled. "You collect junk, Zachariah."

The older man chuckled and gave Luke a wry smile. "*Ja*, I do. But not all of it is junk. Some of it just needs a little elbow grease and a knowing hand to set it to rights. I've heard you keep your father's equipment in tiptop shape."

Luke grimaced inwardly. He did now, but he hadn't always been so diligent. An accident in which his oldest brother had been seriously injured made Luke realize how he had failed his family yet again. Now, he took every step of his work seriously. "I try to keep things in working order."

Zachariah leaned forward. "I want to get my new hardware store open the Monday after Christmas. It's almost finished. After that, I want to get this place in order over the winter. I want it ready for a farm sale in the spring. It's time to get rid of it all."

"That's a tall order." Zachariah owned numerous sheds and buildings crammed to the rafters with all manner of stuff. Clearing it out would be a monumental task.

"I know it's a tall order. That's why I'm looking for help. My boys and I can't do it alone. Roy likes machinery and hardware. He has a gift for it. That's why I want the hardware store finished. He'll run it one day, but he doesn't have the skill to get all of my broken-down machinery working. I'd like to hire you to help me for the next few months."

"I already have a job."

"Surely your father could spare you a few days a week. That's all I'm asking for. A few days a week to look over what I have and see what can be repaired and fix it if you can."

"I think Emma would rather you ask someone else."

"Your breakup was a long time ago. It's water under the bridge to her."

Zachariah might see it that way, but Luke wasn't so sure Emma did. "I don't think it would be a good idea."

Zachariah stared down at his hands for a long moment. When he looked up, Luke saw desperation in his eyes. "I've been remiss in not putting money aside for Emma's dowry. Time just went by too fast. What I get from the sale of my machinery will go to her. She'll marry soon. I don't want her going to a new husband empty-handed. I wouldn't ask you if it wasn't important. What do you say? Can you give me a hand?"

Emma was getting married? Luke shouldn't have been surprised, but he was. Emma was old enough and a fine woman, but it still came as something of a shock. It was hard to imagine her as someone's wife, but she deserved happiness. He wanted her to be happy.

Would helping secure her dowry make up in some small way for his treatment of her in the past? If so, then maybe he could finally put away that guilt.

Tears streamed down Emma's face as she leaned against her bedroom door. She didn't even like Luke anymore. So why did the thought of him risking his life for a chunk of metal turn her blood ice-cold?

He had risked his life to save Roy, too, and she hadn't bothered to thank him.

His bravery she could admire, but she couldn't bear his foolhardiness. He hadn't changed. He would always be the same reckless man who broke her heart.

Rubbing her eyes with both hands, she faced the sad truth. She still went soft inside when

Luke smiled at her. For some unknown reason, he still had a hold on her heart.

Until she remembered how irresponsible he was. Why couldn't she get over this silly school-girl infatuation with him?

Sure, he was a fine-looking man with broad shoulders, slender hips and blond hair that curled just enough to make a girl want to comb it into order with her fingers. There were plenty of nice-looking men in her community, but none of them affected her the way Luke did. Her feelings didn't change the fact that he had gone to prison for dealing drugs after he left the Amish.

It was wrong of her to hold any man's past against him, but she couldn't forget the way he had brushed aside her tender heart when she offered to give up everything and leave with him that night so many years ago. She'd learned a bitter lesson. Luke didn't care about anyone but himself.

She thought she loved him then, but it hadn't been true love. It had been a foolish teenage crush. He had been right to reject her. Now, she knew better than to believe he cared.

Scrubbing her cheeks vigorously to erase the past and the traces of her tears, Emma paced the confines of her small bedroom and struggled to regain her composure. It wasn't just Luke. It was everything. Her father's illness, his desire for her to marry quickly, finding out her brother was ten times more foolhardy than she believed possible—it all added up to a burden too big to carry alone. Luke Bowman's arrival today was simply the straw that broke the camel's back.

And she was a weak camel to begin with. She sat down on the edge of her bed, wishing she could start the day all over again and have it turn out differently.

A gentle tap at her door proved that wasn't going to happen. "Emma?"

"Come in."

Her father peeked around the door. "Are you all right?"

"*Nee*, I'm not. How can I be after your sad news today?"

He entered the room and sat down on the chair against the far wall. Leaning forward, he braced his elbows on his knees. "You will be fine. You are so much like your mother. She was a strong woman, too."

He was wrong. Emma wasn't strong, but he was being brave in the face of his illness. She could do no less. She would pretend to be brave. For him. "What are we going to do with Roy? He's gone too far this time. He could have been killed. Alvin could have been killed. I think you should tell them how ill you are. Maybe that will shock them into behaving."

"They will learn of it soon enough. Let them

be boys for a few more weeks. Perhaps Roy's dunking in the river has taught him a lesson."

At sixteen, Roy was in his *rumspringa*, the years between childhood and adulthood when Amish youth were free to experience the outside world before they were baptized. Once an Amish man or woman chose to be baptized, they embraced the strict rules of the Amish faith, rejecting the outside world forever. If they chose to remain a part of the English world before baptism, they would be able to do so without being shunned by her church group, although not all Amish churches were so open-minded.

Emma had left her *rumspringa* behind at twenty and joined the faithful that same year. She knew Luke had yet to make that decision. He had been living Amish for a year and a half, ever since his release from prison, but he hadn't taken his vows. At twenty-five, his family and the congregation would soon begin pressuring him to make a choice. He couldn't stay on the fence forever. It was time to declare his intentions. Was he going to be *Englisch* or Amish?

She forced herself to stop thinking about him. "I pray you are right and Roy has learned his lesson, but he is hardheaded."

"Like I was. There's an old Amish proverb my father was fond of using. 'Experience is a hard teacher. She gives the test first, then the lesson afterward.'"

"At least Alvin may not follow him so willingly in the future." Alvin was a sensitive boy and not prone to troublemaking unless Roy put him up to it.

"Alvin looks up to Roy as only a younger brother can. It will take more than this incident to tarnish Roy's image in Alvin's eyes."

Her father was probably right. "Did you look up to your older brother in such a fashion?"

Zachariah chuckled. "Your hair would turn gray if you knew half the things my brother, William, and I pulled when we were their ages."

She giggled, amazed she could smile after all that she had learned. "You should go and visit him." Her uncle and his wife along with her father's sister had remained in Missouri when her father moved to Ohio twenty years ago. He had been to visit them only once in all that time.

"Before it's too late, you mean? Don't look so sad. You're right. I should go. Perhaps I will after the New Year. Until then, I have a lot to do here."

Besides farming, her father had always planned to open a hardware business that catered to a few of his Amish neighbors with things like lanterns, nuts, bolts and his prized key-cutting machine that was powered by an ancient diesel generator. Only the shell of the building had been completed. The rest of the things he had collected over the years were junk in her eyes, but occasionally someone needed a part for a broken bailer and Zachariah Swartzentruber was the man to see. He had five bailers in various stages of rust sitting in a long shed he'd built to house them. He never came home from market day empty-handed.

Tears pricked her eyes again. What would she do without him? The doctor had to be wrong. "The boys and I will help with whatever you need."

"I know you will. I want to get my store finished and stocked by Christmas. I have loads of things just waiting to be put out on shelves."

His store was a room he'd built off the side of the house. The roof was on and the walls were framed, but that was all. His shelves were nothing more than long boards stored in the shed alongside the rusting bailers. "Roy and Alvin can help you finish the store."

"I need more help than they can give me. My hands are getting weak, and I can't swing a hammer the way I once did. I need a man's help."

"You're not going to ask Wayne Hochstetler, are you?" The idea of seeing him daily while the work was completed was troubling. What if she didn't like him enough to walk out with him? How could she face him day after day knowing he was sizing her up to be his wife?

"*Nee,* for if Wayne has his mind on courting you, he might not be any use to me. A lovesick fellow often makes a poor worker."

"Then there are a number of young men who should suit your needs nicely. How much will this cost?"

He rose and cupped her cheek with his hand. "Don't worry your head about it, daughter. Buy the material for a new dress, and let me worry about the money."

"All right." She smiled for him.

"That's my girl." He started to leave the room.

"I'll put an ad for a hired man in the newspaper tomorrow."

"No need. I've already hired someone. He starts on Monday."

Her heart dropped like a rock and she closed her eyes. *Please, please, please, don't let it be him.*

"Who did you hire, *Daed*?"

Chapter Three

"I don't feel so *goot*. I don't think I'm ready to go home."

Luke suppressed a smile at Roy's downcast expression as he sat on the edge of the boy's bed the following morning. Roy looked less like a drowned rat today and more like a fella ready to get up to mischief as soon as Rebecca let him out of bed. Both of them knew better than to make that move without her permission. Luke's sister-in-law was a force to be reckoned with. She and Emma were cut from the same cloth.

Why hadn't Rebecca mentioned that Emma was seeing someone? While most Amish sweethearts kept their relationship a tightly guarded secret from the community until the banns were read a few weeks before the wedding, family members usually knew what was going on when a couple became serious. Zachariah's announcement yesterday had hit Luke like a ton of bricks, although he wasn't sure why.

That was a lie. He knew why. Emma held a place in his heart that no other woman had been able to fill.

She should marry. Wasn't that why he had stepped aside all those years ago? Because he wanted her to be happy? He wanted her to build a life in the Amish community where they had grown up. Emma belonged here. She embraced the Amish way of life. It was something he had never been able to do.

All through the rough times when he was on drugs and then behind bars, he imagined Emma living a contented life. He was able to find comfort in that. It had soothed the pain of knowing how poorly he'd treated her. His words that night had been cruel, but they had been for her own good. He knew how much her family was going to need her. He had learned her mother didn't have long to live, but he had been forbidden to tell anyone, even Emma.

Roy plucked at the covers. "I think I should stay here another day or two."

"You're fine. You're just afraid of what your *daed* is gonna do."

"Not *daed*. Emma. She has a way of looking at you that makes you feel two inches tall."

"I've seen that look. Your *daed* didn't seem well when I saw him yesterday."

"He's been feeling poorly for a spell, but he saw the doctor yesterday. I'm sure he'll be better soon."

"Until then, I reckon that means he needs you and your brother's help more than ever with the farm chores."

Roy glanced from beneath his lashes at Luke. "Was he mad at Alvin?"

"A bit. Emma more so."

"There's no surprise." Roy rolled his eyes, forcing Luke to hide another grin.

"Mostly they're thankful both you boys survived. It was a dumb stunt."

Roy scowled. "Micah and I watched you ride a snowmobile up and down that river a few years ago."

"It was a dumb stunt when I did it, too. Micah who?"

"Micah Yoder. We thought it looked like mighty *goot* fun. He would have enjoyed it."

"I'm sure he would until he ended up in the water. Not so much fun then, was it? It could easily have been your brother lying here in your place. Or worse. You know that, don't you?"

A stoic expression settled on Roy's face. "*Ja.* I know."

Luke waited a few moments to let that thought soak in. "Your father mentioned he wants to get some of his equipment ready to sell in the spring. He asked for my help to repair some of his machinery. He offered to hire me for a couple of months."

Roy's face split into a wide grin as he scooted up in bed and leaned against the headboard. "Are you gonna take the job? That would be *wunderbar*."

"I'm glad you like the idea." Luke still didn't know what had come over him. He never should have accepted Zachariah's offer. He hadn't even spoken to his own father yet.

"I have so many things to ask you, Luke. You know everything about life in the city and about the things an Amish guy needs to do if he wants to live English. You can teach me that stuff, can't you? I'm a quick learner."

A chuckle made Luke look over his shoulder. His brother Samuel stood in the doorway. Samuel's face still bore the faint scars of the burns he had suffered when their gasoline generator exploded. Luke's carelessness had contributed to the accident. He knew Samuel had forgiven him, but he had a hard time forgiving himself. His one consolation was that Samuel's need for a nurse after the accident had brought Rebecca into their lives. Samuel considered Rebecca's love well worth the pain he had suffered.

Samuel advanced into the room. "Luke can teach you how to get into trouble anywhere, Roy. Amish or *Englisch* trouble, it doesn't matter to him. I'd avoid his company if I were you."

"He sure saved my hide yesterday."

"And the lesson learned from this?" Luke prompted.

"Don't take a snowmobile out on the river no matter how thick the ice looks."

Luke shook his head. He recognized a restless spirit in Roy. It was the same restlessness that had filled him at that age. "The lesson is to stay off snowmobiles and all *Englisch* machines."

Roy cast him a sheepish look. "I doubt I'll get the chance to ride one again since I almost ruined Mr. Morgan's."

Luke thumped his finger into Roy's chest. "It serves you right. Just so you know, Jim Morgan came by to collect his machine. His brother isn't going to be riding for a while, either. Jim wasn't happy to hear Brian let you boys ride off without adult supervision."

Samuel chuckled again. "That is the pot calling the kettle black. You and Jim were always up to no good when the adults weren't looking. He's the one who taught you to drive a car when you didn't have a license."

Luke frowned at his brother. "You're not helping, Samuel."

His brother laughed again. "*Daed* wants to see you downstairs."

Luke nodded and rose to his feet. "Okay. I'll check on you later, Roy. Stay in bed or Rebecca will have your head on a platter and mine, too."

Luke followed Samuel out of the spare bedroom. In the hallway, Samuel gave him a sidelong glance. "You took a job working for Zachariah? You're joking, right?"

"I don't know what happened. I opened my mouth to refuse, but that wasn't what came out. I agreed to a part-time job for a few months. Maybe more."

"What were you thinking? Did sticking your head under the ice freeze your pea-size brain?"

"Maybe so." Until recently, Samuel's teasing would have made Luke fighting mad, but these days the brothers had come to understand and respect each other.

"There's no maybe about it. Then again, it will get you out from under my feet."

"Sammy, you'll come crawling to find me the second that finicky planer jams again, begging me to fix it."

"On bended knee. You're the only one who can coax that machine to do its job. Zachariah might have made a smart move getting you to help him."

Working for Zachariah was a bad idea for so many reasons. Number one—Emma would hate having him around.

Number two—he already had a job working for his father in the family's woodworking and gift shop. He wasn't sure his father could spare him.

Number three—Emma would hate having him around.

His parents were sitting at the kitchen table when he came downstairs. The fact that his mother wasn't offering him food proved it was going to be a serious talk. His father folded his hands in front of him. "What is this about you taking another job?"

Luke looked back and forth between them. "How did you find out?"

"Rebecca spoke to Emma this morning."

Luke shoved his hands in the pockets of his pants. The Amish might not use telephones, but that didn't stop news from spreading like wildfire. "Zachariah talked me into a part-time job working for him. It was a mistake. I'll tell him I've changed my mind or that you can't spare me."

"What sort of job is it?" his mother asked.

"He wants help finishing his hardware store before Christmas. It would be mostly simple carpentry, stocking shelves and taking inventory. I don't think the man knows half of what he has stashed away."

Samuel rubbed a hand over his new beard, the one he'd started growing after his marriage, and scratched at his chin. "Luke, you suggested that we add a hardware section to our gift shop. I've been seriously considering it. Won't Zachariah be in competition with us?"

Luke's father snorted. "In all the years I've known him, Zachariah Swartzentruber has rarely finished a project he started. He won't become our competition. I doubt he'll ever complete his store."

"Isaac, that is unkind," his mother said with a sharp-eyed scowl at her mate. "Our neighbor has asked Luke for help. What do you think, Samuel? Can we spare Luke for a few weeks? Don't forget, your father and I will be gone to Florida for a month after Christmas."

Samuel fixed his gaze on Luke. "Will you have to notify your parole officer that you have a new job? Working and living here was one of the conditions of your early release, wasn't it?"

It wasn't common knowledge that he was still on parole. Only a few people outside the immediate family knew. His parents didn't like to discuss anything to do with his time in prison. He had caused them enough embarrassment in the community. He was surprised his brother mentioned it in front of them. "I'm not moving, and it would be in addition to my work here, so it shouldn't make a difference."

Samuel propped his hands on his hips. "If a neighbor needs help, we must give it. We can spare you, Luke. We're caught up on our Christmas orders for both the gift shop and the woodshop. Unless we get more than a few rush orders, Timothy, Noah and I can handle your work. As long as you can make any equipment repairs we need."

"You don't have to pick up my slack. I'll tell Zachariah I can't do it."

"How is Emma?" his mother asked with a look of innocence.

Suspicious at the abrupt change of topic, Luke shrugged. "Fine as far as I know. Ask Rebecca. She'll know more than I do."

"Won't it be hard for Emma to have you at her home? The two of you were close once. She was broken-hearted when you left."

His father shook his head. "That was a long time ago, *mudder.* They were *kinder.*"

Luke avoided his mother's sharp gaze. He and Emma hadn't been children, but they had been too young to know what love was. He tried for an offhand tone. "I'm sure Emma couldn't care less if I work with her father or not."

"You are right about that." A cold voice he recognized came from behind him.

He spun around to see Emma and Rebecca standing in the doorway to the living room. They must have come in through the back door, for both women wore their traveling bonnets and cloaks. Emma had a fixed smile pasted on her face. Rebecca shook her head and glared at him.

His mother rose to her feet. "Emma, how nice to see you. If this arrangement is all right with you, then it's okay with us. Luke can work for your father."

Great. Now he was stuck with the job. Maybe it was for the best. Maybe if he and Emma spent some time together they could put the past to rest and start over. He wasn't expecting friendship, but he hoped for something more civil than the icy stare he was getting at the moment.

"How is Roy?" Rebecca asked, pulling off her bonnet.

"Goot," Samuel said. "He's been a better patient than I was."

She laughed. "That wouldn't take much. Come, Emma, I'll show you up to his room. He was very blessed that Luke was able to reach him under the ice and pull him out. I hope he knows that."

Emma pulled off her bonnet, too, and dropped her gaze to her hands. "I haven't thanked you for saving his life, Luke."

"You're welcome." He'd dive in a freezing river again if she would just smile at him—say she forgave him.

She didn't. She left the room and followed Rebecca upstairs.

"You can't still be mad at him after all these years."

"I don't know what you mean." Emma avoided eye contact with her cousin.

"I saw the look you gave Luke. If your eyes were a frying pan and Luke was an egg, he'd be burned to a crisp."

"You're being silly. He's right. I couldn't care less about what he does or where he goes." And that was exactly how she would behave from now on. She wasn't about to be known as a weak-willed old maid carrying a torch for someone who didn't love her.

"I'm beginning to think you care more about Luke than you're letting on." Rebecca paused to knock on a door halfway down the hall.

"Come in." Roy's muffled voice smote Emma's conscience. She should be worrying about him, not about what Rebecca or anyone else thought of her relationship with Luke.

Emma pushed open the door. Her brother was sitting up in bed with a checkerboard on his legs. Noah, the youngest Bowman son, was sitting beside his bed on a chair. He looked up and smiled. "You have fine timing. He was about to beat me."

"For the third straight game," Roy added.

Emma marched up to the bed and propped her hands on her hips. "For someone who cheated death, you look pretty good to me."

He sank back against the pillows. "I'm still shook up, *shveshtah*."

"I hope you are. Your foolishness could have put you in an early grave."

Rebecca came to her side, her arms crossed

over her chest. "He looks a lot better than he did yesterday."

Emma bent to capture his face between her hands. She planted a kiss on his forehead, which he promptly wiped away. "He looks *wunderbar*. Can I take him home?"

"Maybe. I need to examine him first. Hold your arms straight out to your sides, Roy."

He did. She nodded and made a small sound of approval. "Does that hurt?"

"Nee."

"Goot. Open wide and stick out your tongue, but keep your arms up." He did and she bent closer to examine him. "Now, flap your arms up and down."

He shot her a quizzical look, but did as she asked.

Rebecca glanced at Emma, but couldn't keep a straight face. "Does he look like a baby bird getting ready to fly the coop?"

Emma nodded. "He does."

"Then I think he's ready to be released." Rebecca took a step back as Roy glared at her. Noah started laughing and almost fell off his chair.

"Ha! Ha! Very funny, cousin." Roy tossed his covers back, sending the checkers flying.

"That's a good one, Rebecca." Noah slapped his thigh and kept laughing. "I'm gonna call him Birdie Roy from now on. A fella needs a nickname for sure. Birdie Roy. Tweet, tweet."

Roy fumed at Noah. "I'm going to get dressed. Where are my clothes?"

"*Mamm* washed them. I'll fetch them for you unless you've got a hankering to go sit on the clothesline for a spell. Tweet, tweet." Noah left the room, still chuckling.

"Now look what you did. I'll never hear the end of this." Roy folded his arms over his chest.

"See you later, little cousin." Laughing, too, Rebecca waved and left the room.

Emma gave her brother a quick hug. "I'm so glad you're all right. Forgive our teasing."

"I guess I have to. But if Noah keeps this up, he's gonna get a snowball in the face the next time he steps outside."

"Vengeance is not our way," Emma chided. Roy was still such a child. He would need to grow up so fast once their father was gone. It hurt to think of the pain he would soon go through when he learned the news. Maybe her father was right. Maybe the boys deserved this one last happy Christmas. She would do that for them.

"I'll put a handful of snow down his back if it will make you feel better," Luke offered from the doorway. "That's not vengeance, it's brotherly love." He came into the room with a bundle of clothes in his hands. "*Mamm* sent me up with these."

Emma's heart did its funny skip, but she quickly ignored the sensation. "*Danki*, Luke.

As soon as he is dressed, I'll take him off your hands. My buggy is outside."

She left the room so her brother could have some privacy. Luke followed her into the hall and stopped close beside her. Too close. She could see the gray flecks in his blue eyes when she looked into his face. The soap he used accentuated his own unique masculine scent. It must be one of Rebecca's. She made a number of herb-infused bars that smelled delightful. Emma was sure she hadn't smelled this one before. She breathed in deeply, not wanting to exhale.

How foolish was that? As soon as she decided she wasn't going to care what Luke did, she couldn't stop thinking about him.

"Tell your father that I'll be over first thing Monday morning."

"All right."

He hesitated, then said, "I don't want to make things uncomfortable for you, Emma. Are you sure you are okay with this?"

He looked truly concerned about her. How was she supposed to answer him?

"Luke, it doesn't matter to me if you work for my father. So long as you keep true to the teachings of our faith."

His eyes went from warm to frosty in a heartbeat. "You mean stay away from drugs."

If he was angry with her, so much the better.

"You know what I mean. Our faith has many rules, and you like bending the rules."

"What if I say that I've changed? Would you believe me?"

"I would pray fervently that is true."

"Not exactly what I wanted to hear."

She crossed her arms tightly over her chest. "It's the best I can do."

"Then maybe I should tell your father I've changed my mind." He pulled back. A shadow slipped across his eyes.

Was it pain? Had she hurt him? That was never her intention. "I'm sorry."

"Don't be. It's best to get our feelings out in the open. I'll speak to your father tomorrow."

This wasn't about her feelings. It was about her father and what he needed. "*Nee*, Luke. *Daed* can use the help. He's not been well. You would be doing him a great favor if you came to work for him."

"There are a lot of fellows he could hire to help."

"But you understand machines. You will know what can be fixed and what is junk fit only for scrap. At least he'll make a little money off that."

"And making money is important, isn't it? Of course it is. What woman wants to go into a marriage empty-handed?"

She drew back in shock. "Marriage? Who said anything about marriage?"

"Zachariah mentioned it in passing."

Her cheeks burned with humiliation. Was her father trying to force her hand by spreading the story that she was about to wed? She pressed her lips together. "He shouldn't have said anything. Nothing is decided."

"I understand. Amish couples like to keep things secret. Don't worry. I won't say anything."

"Danki." But she was going to have plenty to say to her father.

Luke's gaze softened. "Whoever he is, Emma, he's a fortunate man."

His eyes pulled at her heartstrings, making her long to move into his arms and rest her head on his shoulder the way she once had. She licked her suddenly dry lips.

Roy came out of the bedroom. "I'm ready."

Emma tore her gaze away from Luke. "I have to go."

She followed her brother down the hall. At the stairwell, she glanced back and saw Luke was still watching her. Was it a trick of the light, or did she see regret in his eyes?

Chapter Four

On Saturday afternoon, Emma traveled to the home of her friend, Lillian Keim. Lillian was the teacher at Alvin's school, but the two women had been friends since the cradle. It had been Lillian who listened to Emma pour out her grief when Luke left. Lillian's family had moved away not long afterward, leaving Emma to tell her friend how well she was recovering through letters. It was easier to bend the truth in writing. Then, two years ago, Lillian, her parents, her brother and her new little sister had returned to Bowmans Crossing so that Lillian could take the teacher's post that had opened up. Emma was delighted to find they picked up their friendship right where they left off.

As Emma stopped her horse in front of Lillian's house, she recognized her cousin Rebecca's buggy tied to the hitching rail. The three of them were the planning committee for the school's Christmas program.

"Hello," Emma called as she entered the house.

"We're in the living room," Lillian called back.

Emma crossed the kitchen and turned the corner to see Rebecca and Rebecca's mother, Ina Fisher, sitting on the sofa with cups of tea in their hands. Lillian sat in a chair facing them. She gestured toward another chair beside her. "Come and sit here. I was just telling Rebecca and your *aenti* your news. I hope you don't mind."

"What news? Hello *Aenti* Ina. I wasn't expecting you to join us. How are you?" Emma approached the couch and kissed her aunt on the cheek.

Ina gave a long-suffering sigh. "Not bad for a woman my age. You young people don't want to hear about my arthritis or my sciatic pain."

Rebecca winked, and Emma knew she had to say something. "I'm so sorry you are suffering, *Aenti*. I must say, you bear up remarkably well. I don't know how you manage."

Apparently mollified, her aunt smiled a little. "*Danki*, child. I try."

Emma sat in the chair next to Lillian. "Were you talking about Roy's escapade? He's fine, although I fear he may not have learned his lesson."

"Lillian told us that Luke Bowman is working for your father. That must be odd for you." Ina took a sip of her tea, but her sharp eyes never left Emma's face.

"I don't find it odd at all. Why should I?" Emma kept her face carefully blank. Ina was well-known as a gossip in the community. Emma didn't want to fuel new speculation about Luke and herself.

Ina shrugged. "No reason, other than I do wonder if he will be a bad influence on Roy."

Rebecca gave her mother a speaking glance. "Luke is not a bad influence on anyone. Shame on you for implying otherwise."

Ina pressed a hand to her heart. "I didn't mean to speak ill of him. Gracious, no."

"I thought not." Rebecca sipped her tea, but her frown remained.

"I was merely thinking that Roy is the age when he would find Luke's prior life exciting."

Lillian shook her head. "Prison can hardly be considered exciting."

"Not to us, of course," Ina conceded.

"Not to Roy, either," Emma stated firmly, but she wondered if she spoke the truth. No matter how hard she tried to keep Roy from straying, she wasn't sure she could. As Luke had at his age, her brother seemed determined to live an English life.

Rebecca set her teacup in the saucer on the small table in front of her. "We're here to plan the Christmas program, not to gossip about my husband's brother."

Lillian giggled. "Where's the fun in that? If you will step outside, we'll be happy to talk about you instead."

Emma chuckled. "I hope the art of gossip isn't a lesson you are teaching our *kinder* at school."

"I'm afraid it is a lesson learned more readily at home than at school." Rebecca gave her mother a pointed look.

Ina put her teacup down, too. "Let us hear your ideas for the program this year, Lillian. This Thursday is the first of December, so we need to get moving."

Lillian opened a notebook she had sitting on her lap. "My thought was to tell the Christmas story from the shepherds' point of view. They were, after all, the first to hear the good news of our Savior's birth. Emma, I'm sure Alvin told you I want him to sing a solo. He has a remarkably beautiful voice. He's not keen on the idea. I hope you can encourage him to do it. I don't want to force him."

"He does sing well," Ina admitted. "What song did you have in mind for him?"

"'The First Noel.'"

Rebecca clasped her hands together. "It's a lovely Christmas song and one of my favorites."

"Will the other children have a chance to sing,

too?" Emma asked. Alvin wouldn't want to be the only one.

Lillian leaned forward. "Oh, absolutely. Since we are telling the story of the shepherds, we could start with the hymn 'While Shepherds Watched Their Flocks.' I will have one of the fourth-grade girls be the angel that appears to them. How many shepherds do you think I should have?"

Rebecca shrugged. "It doesn't say how many there were in the Bible. I think four or five would be a good number."

"I agree. Then I will have the first-and second-grade girls be the host of angels. Eight of them in all. We'll also need to choose someone to play Joseph and Mary. Who would like to help with the costumes?" Lillian glanced hopefully around the room.

"I can," Emma said.

"What about scenery or sets?" Rebecca asked.

Lillian folded her notebook closed. "Timothy Bowman has expressed an interest in helping with that."

Ina frowned. "He doesn't have a child in school."

"His niece, Hannah, is a new student with us this year." Lillian smoothed her skirt, keeping her eyes downcast.

Emma caught Rebecca's eye. Was Timothy interested in courting their friend? Rebecca's expression said she had no idea.

The sound of the front door opening was followed by childish laughter. Lillian's little sister came hurrying into the room. "Lilly, I got a Christmas present for you, but I can't tell you what it is."

Emma smiled at the girl. Born with dwarfism, Amanda was three years old and a happy, active child. Many Amish families had members who were little people. Lillian's family was thankful that Amanda had none of the health problems that often accompanied the disorder.

Lillian's mother, Marietta Keim, came into the room and greeted everyone. She leaned down to her daughter. "Amanda, your sister has visitors. You shouldn't interrupt."

"I'm sorry, but I had to tell her about her present."

Lillian pulled her close. "I'm so glad you did. I shall be on pins and needles the entire month wondering what it is."

Marietta held out her hand. "Come help me gather the eggs, Amanda."

"Okay." She rushed to her mother's side, and they both went out.

The women spent the next half hour working on the details of the program. After Rebecca and her mother left, Lillian crossed her arms and stared at Emma. "Well?"

"Well, what?"

"Luke Bowman working for your father. That can't be good."

"It doesn't matter to me what Luke does or where he works."

"It used to matter a lot. You can't take up with him again, Emma."

"Who said I was?"

"He'll break your heart again. Men like him always do."

There were no other men like Luke Bowman. He was one of a kind.

She rose from her chair and went to stare out the window. "I'm not getting involved with him. He's not interested in me. He's been home over a year. If he wanted to walk out with me, he would have asked ages ago, and I would have turned him down. My father is pushing me to wed someone else."

Lillian sat bolt upright. "What? Who? Why?"

"Wayne Hochstetler. Because it's time I married. I'm not getting any younger."

"We are barely twenty-five. We're not old maids. Not yet."

"I don't want to be an old maid, and neither do you."

"That's where you're wrong. I intend to remain single, but we are talking about you. Are you walking out with Wayne?"

"Not yet. This is something his father and my

father cooked up between them, but apparently Wayne is on the lookout for a wife."

Lillian sat back. "He would be with such a young daughter to raise. It might be a good match, Emma. He's a steady fellow, hardworking and not bad looking. He has a nice farm. You would have a ready-made family."

Emma couldn't come up with a thing against him except he wasn't Luke. "If you think it's such a good deal, why don't *you* marry him?"

"I told you. I'm going to be single and teach school all my days. I love it."

She rose and went to stand at Emma's side. Slipping an arm across Emma's shoulders, Lillian drew her close. "We have been friends a long time. I remember how upset you were when Luke left and didn't take you with him. I thank God he had that much sense, but I could cheerfully horsewhip him for the pain he caused you."

"I didn't know you were such a violent person."

"Okay, I wouldn't horsewhip a bug, but I could send Luke Bowman to stand in the corner for the rest of his life."

Emma managed a smile. "I can see you have the makings of a great teacher. Please don't worry about me. I'm okay. Having Luke work for my father has stirred up old memories, but that's all they are. Memories. I live in the here and now. He can't hurt me."

"I pray you are right."

Emma prayed that she was, too.

Sunday was the off Sunday when there wasn't a church meeting. The Amish had church every other week. Luke's family remained at home that day. His father led a quiet morning of prayer and Bible reading. Luke tried to keep his mind on the words his father spoke, but his thoughts kept drifting to Emma and the look on her face before she left with Roy. There had been something in her eyes when she gazed at him. Was it possible that she still cared after the way he'd treated her?

He should have found a gentler way to break it off between them. He had known that she loved him. He had loved her, too, although he never told her that. His feelings for Emma had frightened the wits out of him. Marriage would have tied him to the Amish life forever. She never understood his need to be free from his family's expectations and from everything Amish that had stifled him. Drugs had given him the feeling of freedom he craved, but only for a while.

If he had allowed her to come with him, it would have ruined her life. Leaving her behind was the only good thing he'd ever done for her. Did she understand that?

It didn't seem likely, but there had been something in the way she looked at him that gave him hope.

Hope for what?

What was it that he wanted from her? To rekindle their teenage romance? He was too old and too jaded to think that was possible.

Forgiveness? He craved that, but he didn't expect it. How could he when he had never explained why he left her.

Did he hope for a new friendship with her? Maybe.

None of it mattered if he wasn't staying in Bowmans Crossing. The closer the time came for him to make a decision about staying the less certain he became of what he was going to do. From the moment he got out of jail, he had been struggling to fit in, to find where he belonged. Once his parole was up, he would be truly free. Free to leave. Free to stay. Which did he want?

His whole life he had rebelled against the strict and narrow Amish world he'd been born into. He'd never felt as if he were a part of it. Only sweet Emma had made it bearable. Her shy smiles, her adorable laugh, those tender stolen kisses. Oh yes, Emma had tempted him to stay, but her love hadn't been enough.

Luke had grown to envy his *Englisch* friend, Jim Morgan. It had seemed that Jim and his buddies had a million choices. They had money to spend, cars to take them anywhere they wanted to go. There had been parties, loud music, fun and later there had been drugs, too. The Amish singings and picnics Emma wanted to attend seemed dull as dirt in comparison.

Always a risk taker, Luke dove headfirst into a lifestyle that had seemed too good to be true. And it was.

The occasional party drugs hadn't been enough after a while. He sought escape more often, and one of Jim's buddies supplied what he needed. Although Luke had believed he could quit whenever he wanted, he hadn't been able to do so. In the end, he rejected Emma's love, lost the respect of his family and his self-respect, too.

And he had no one to blame but himself.

Now, the Lord had led him full circle. He was back at the same crossroads. Stay or go? Which would be best for his family? Their unwavering support and love had given his life new meaning, but did he belong here?

If only he could be sure he wouldn't fail them again.

At noon, his mother prepared a light meal, and afterward Luke walked down to the riverbank behind the house. The water was frozen a few feet out from the shore, but it was open in a winding path down the center of the river. A flock of mallard ducks flew up from the open water, circled and landed farther downstream, quacking their displeasure at being disturbed. He tossed a stick into the water and watched it drift away.

"What is troubling you, *brudder*?"

He recognized Joshua's voice and turned to see all four of his brothers walking down to join him. "I'm not troubled."

Joshua stopped a few feet away and folded his arms. "I've heard that before. I didn't buy it then and I'm not buying it now."

"What gives?" Noah asked. At twenty, he was the youngest of the Bowman sons and the least Amish looking with his short brown hair, English clothes and blue ball cap. He was taking advantage of his *rumspringa* to enjoy some non-Amish activities, but Luke knew Noah had every intention of joining the faith in a few years.

"Are you thinking of leaving us again?" Trust Samuel to get straight to the point.

"We all want you to stay," Timothy added quietly. "I hope you know that."

Luke nodded, unable to speak until he swallowed the lump in his throat. "I know you want me here."

Samuel laid a hand on Luke's shoulder. "But?"

"But I wish I knew for certain that I could stay."

Joshua tipped his hat back. "Luke, no one but you can make that decision. Why do you think you should leave?"

Joshua had believed he could convince Luke to return to the family. He had tracked Luke down and found him selling drugs to support his habit. Shame and guilt kept Luke from accepting Joshua's help. Unfortunately, they both were swept up in a drug raid, and his innocent brother had been sent to prison, too. Amazingly, Joshua didn't harbor any ill will toward him.

Luke stared at the ground. "I should leave because I'm a drug addict and a convict. How many Amish fellows can say that?"

"Ex-addict. Ex-convict," Samuel said sternly.

Luke glanced at him. "Am I? Therein lies my dilemma. I'm not using drugs now. I don't want to go back to prison, and failing a drug test would put me there in a heartbeat. I'm straight now, but once prison isn't hanging over my head, will I give in and start using again?"

Samuel shook him by the shoulders. "You won't."

Luke pulled away from his brother. "You don't know that because I don't know that."

The fear of falling back into that life hovered over him every day. He wasn't strong. He'd failed before. He could fail again. Why was he so different from his siblings? Looking into their faces, he knew they didn't understand his fears. How could they? They were all so sure of their place in life.

Forcing a smile, he hooked a thumb toward the house. "Why don't I beat you at a game of checkers, Samuel? That always makes me feel better."

Noah shoved his hands in the pockets of his

jacket. "*Daed* has already challenged him. You'll have to wait and play the winner."

"Go on, then. I'll be up in a minute."

His brothers walked reluctantly up the hill. He threw one more stick in the water and followed. As he entered the back garden gate, he saw Joshua's wife, Mary, sitting on a bench. She had her eyes closed and her face raised to the afternoon sun. Several of the gourd birdhouses he had painted added color to the winter landscape. "I know how you're feeling, Luke."

"I doubt that." He took a seat beside her.

"You feel lost. Others seem to know exactly what they want out of life and you still don't know what you're seeking. For two cents, you'd put a boat on the river, get in it and drift away until you reached the sea or sank." She opened her eyes and looked at him. "Am I close?"

"Amazingly so."

"I was like you before I had Hannah."

Luke knew some of her story. Mary had left the Amish as a young girl, ended up with a man who used and then abandoned her when he found out she was pregnant. Alone and on the streets, she was taken in by a drug dealer named Dunbar, who planned to sell her baby when it was born. She gave birth alone and managed to hide Hannah from him in an Amish buggy, leaving a note with her child that she would come back for her. What she hadn't known was the buggy belonged to two teenage Amish boys who panicked when they discovered the baby. They left her on the doorstep of the nearest Amish farm. It was only thanks to Miriam Kauffman, an ex-Amish nurse, and Sheriff Nick Bradley that Mary was eventually reunited with her baby, and the drug dealer was sent to prison. Nick and Miriam married and adopted Mary. When Hannah was five, Joshua rescued the mother and child during a tornado and soon fell in love with them both. Once again, it had been Luke's weakness that almost ruined everything for them.

"You are a stronger person than I am, Mary. You've seen how weak I can be. You suffered because of it."

"God gave me someone to make me strong. He gave me Hannah. He will give you the strength you need if you trust Him."

"I don't know that I believe that. I have the feeling that I'm out here on my own. I think He's washed His hands of me. I don't know why you haven't."

"Because Joshua loves you."

"I don't understand that, either. He tried to help me and I pulled him down with me. He spent time in prison because of me. I gave the man who hated you information about you in exchange for drugs when I was in prison."

"You didn't know Kevin Dunbar's intentions. He used you."

"He kidnapped Hannah and could have killed her because of me."

"God, in His great mercy, spared my child. You told the authorities where Dunbar was going once you knew what had happened. Nick got my little girl back because of your help. You were part of God's plan all along, Luke. Don't doubt that."

"I'd feel better about being part of the solution if I hadn't caused the problem. I don't deserve another chance to mess up someone's life." If he stayed, it would happen. To Mary or to Hannah or God forbid to Emma. He would fail them when they needed him most. In his heart of hearts, he knew it.

Mary sighed softly. "I've never told anyone in the family this other than my husband, but I tried to kill myself when I lost Hannah the first time. It was hard to believe God could forgive me for such an act. The truth is God forgave me long before I made that terrible decision. He sent His only Son to die on a cross to save me from my sin. God forgives all of us. I was the one who couldn't forgive myself until I realized that God had sent Joshua to love me in spite of everything. Your sins will be forgiven if you accept the truth of our Savior's sacrifice for you, Luke. Until you accept that and forgive yourself, you won't find happiness here or anywhere."

"It's easier said than done, Mary."

"You're right. It is. But it's possible. Now let's go in. I'm getting cold and your mother was making some hot cocoa." She rose to her feet.

Luke stared at her in amazement. "I hope my brother knows how blessed he is to have found a woman like you, Mary."

She grinned. "I tell him often, so he's not likely to forget."

Luke chuckled. He could hear Emma saying something like that. Emma was a strong woman, too. If only he could undo his past mistakes and make her love him again.

No, he was a fool if he tried to hold on to that hope, but to his dismay, it wouldn't die.

Chapter Five

Luke spent Monday morning prowling through Zachariah's sheds and barn, taking stock of what equipment the man had squirreled away. He found eight chain saws, none of which worked, and a half dozen two-man saws that only needed sharpening; six bailers in various stages of rust; three silage blowers; eighteen carriage wheels; twelve sets of harnesses; four plows; four harrows; fifty-five assorted sizes of horseshoes and a busted corn binder. As he went through, over and around the piles, he made notes in a small spiral notebook. Roy worked with him, but Alvin had school and wouldn't be home until after three o'clock.

Zachariah came out to check on their progress occasionally, but for the most part, he puttered in the half-built hardware store. Luke gained the impression that it was hard for Zachariah to see his holdings being assessed by someone with an eye to selling them. He didn't see hide nor hair of Emma. Was she avoiding him?

Stupid question. Of course she was.

Where they could, Luke and Roy moved Zachariah's hoard to lay it out for better access and to inventory the cardboard boxes and wooden crates filled with gears, bearings, nails and assorted small tools. They were both covered with dust and grease within a few hours.

"I count twenty-three oil lamps complete with shades and wicks in these boxes. Looks like only one shade is cracked." Luke replaced the last lid and moved to tally the rope and tackle hanging on pegs nearby.

"What are these?" Roy asked, pulling a tarp away from a stack of silver-and-blue metal panels in the hayloft of Zachariah's largest barn. Luke suspected the horses' and cattle's need for hay was the only reason this part of the barn hadn't been overtaken yet.

Luke stopped counting the pulleys and puzzled over Roy's find for second. "I think they're solar panels."

"The kind that make electricity?"

"*Ja.* I wonder how your *daed* came by them. I always thought they were expensive to buy."

"He probably traded for them. That's what *Daed* does. He trades for stuff. He rarely buys anything. Could these be used to charge up my cell phone?"

"I'm sure it could, but I don't know how to make it work."

Roy flipped the cover back over the solar array. "I thought you were gonna tell me to get rid of my phone. That's what Emma would say."

"I know a lot of guys your age carry them. You aren't baptized yet, so you don't have to abide by the church rules."

"Emma says I need to. She is always harping about how hard it will be to give up my *Englisch* things later. She says it's better to give them up now before I get attached to them."

"She might have a point. You shouldn't be too hard on your sister. She means well."

"I know. It's just that she tries to be our mother. She's not."

"She's been taking care of you and Alvin since you were little. You can't blame her for wanting to see that you turn out right."

"How I turn out is going to be my decision, not hers."

The boy had a point. No amount of his mother's prayers or pleading had kept Luke home when he was ready to leave. "Once she gets married, she won't have as much time to fuss at you."

Roy's eyebrows shot up. "Emma is getting married?"

"Your *daed* mentioned as much. I figured you knew."

"I thought my sister would be an old maid forever."

"So you don't know who she has been seeing?" Was that odd, or was Roy simply too caught up in his own life to see what was happening under his nose? Luke was ashamed to admit that he had been like that at Roy's age.

"*Nee.* Wow. Who will take care of Alvin?"

"I reckon you and your father can manage."

"I'll be leaving. I mean, one of these days I'm gonna live in the city. That's where all the excitement is."

Luke tensed. "What kind of excitement?"

"Lights, movie theaters, televisions, bars, girls that dress fancy. Micah and I talked a lot about the things we'd see there."

Relaxing a bit, Luke was relieved that Roy hadn't mentioned drugs. "None of it is free. How would you pay for a place with lights and a television?"

"I'll get a job."

"It's not as easy as it sounds." Without the simple basics such as a driver's license and social security card, and with only an eighth-grade education, a decent job was almost impossible to come by. To his deep regret, Luke had chosen the wrong way to make money.

"Is that why you came back, because you couldn't find work?" Roy asked.

Luke hesitated, but decided to tell Roy the

truth. Maybe it would keep him from making the same kind of mistakes. "Living here is a condition of my parole. You knew I went to prison, didn't you?"

Roy shrugged. "Sure. Everyone knows. I think it's cool."

Luke rounded on the boy. "It wasn't cool! I spent a year of my life locked in a cage with men you never want to meet. I made stupid decisions, and people got hurt. I paid the price for that. A lot like your ride on the snowmobile. Only there wasn't anyone standing by to haul my soggy behind to shore. I pulled my brother Joshua into trouble with me, and it was only by the grace of God that we survived."

Roy backed away from Luke's anger. "I'm sorry."

Luke sucked in a deep breath and blew it out, letting his anger flow away with it. "I'm the one who is sorry. Forgive me."

Roy rubbed his hands on his pant legs. "It must have been hard, but it's over now."

"It's not over. I'm not in jail, but I'm still on parole until the end of my sentence. That means I have to report to an *Englisch* parole officer every month. If I don't do what they tell me, I can be sent back to prison."

"I didn't know that."

Another month and then he would truly be a free man. A man able to live his life as he saw fit without reporting to anyone. Without this great shadow hanging over his head.

"You have to understand that the *Englisch* world is much more than lights and movies, Roy. It has a very dark side. You need to think long and hard about what you're leaving, and why you're leaving. If you decide to live *Englisch*, you need to be prepared."

"That's why I'm glad you're here. Where did you stay when you first left?"

Luke cringed at the memory. "In a crummy old motel a few blocks north of the bus station in Cincinnati called the Gray Cat. I had heard that a bunch of ex-Amish kids were staying there. I didn't have a clue about life off the farm let alone how to survive in a dangerous slum. The management charged way too much for those run-down rooms."

The owner had also had unscrupulous contacts eager to employ the underage and unsuspecting youths who desperately needed jobs when their money ran out or was stolen.

"The Gray Cat. That is the kind of stuff I want to learn. I knew you'd help me get out of here."

"Then you are doomed to be disappointed because I'm not going to help you leave. You don't know half the dangers that are out there."

"I'm not staying here. I'll be bored out of my skull for the rest of my life."

"How do you charge your cell phone, anyway?" Luke asked to change the subject. He could see he wasn't getting through to the boy.

Roy looked disappointed, but said, "I have three batteries that I rotate. Fannie Erb has a phone charger that runs off a car battery. Alvin stops by there on his way to school, leaves one with her and picks it up on his way home. If he forgets or school isn't on, I go to Brian Morgan's place. He lets me use his charger for a small price. Well, he used to. I'm not sure he will after I wrecked the snowmobile. If we could get a solar panel running, I know a lot of fellas from our neighboring church group who would pay to use it."

"From Bishop Hochstetler's church? I thought they didn't permit any phones at all. Not even a community phone booth."

"They don't, but some kids have them, anyway. They sure don't want to get caught with one. Bishop Hochstetler had the parents of one kid shunned after he was caught with a phone. The bishop claimed they hadn't raised their son properly."

"Was this your friend Micah?"

Roy nodded. "I was the one who got the phone for him. He gave it up after that. He didn't want his folks punished for the things he did."

"I can understand that."

Every Amish congregation decided on the *Ordnung* for their church. Some were much more conservative than others and their bishops held great sway over the members. Bishop Hochstetler's group was one of the strictest. His church members lived without indoor plumbing or running water. Their children weren't allowed a *rumspringa*, but were all expected to join the church when they came of age. Members were even forbidden to use reflectors on their buggies, including the orange slow-moving vehicle triangle that adorned the back of every buggy in Luke's congregation. Luke didn't agree with their way of thinking, but he respected the people who adhered to the old ways so staunchly.

"Did Micah stop seeing you because of his parents' shunning?"

"*Nee*, not because of that."

Luke was shocked by the sadness in Roy's voice.

Outside, the clanging of a bell signaled the noon meal was ready. Roy started for the ladder. "Emma doesn't like us to keep her waiting. Come on."

Luke stayed rooted to the spot. He'd known this moment was coming, but that didn't make it any easier. He would have to share a meal with Emma and her family. He would have to sit across from her and pretend she didn't set his head spinning like a top. He'd have to pretend it didn't matter that she was thinking about marrying.

Who was the fellow? He was dying to know.

* * *

Emma had her emotions well in hand by the time she rang the dinner bell. Luke's presence was nothing more than a minor annoyance. Nothing of their past relationship remained. She wanted to make sure he got the message in case he thought otherwise.

After everyone had washed up and taken their place at the table, she carried the platter of meat loaf and turnips from the oven and placed it in front of her father. She took her place opposite Luke, folded her hands demurely and prayed silently.

Her father cleared his throat to signal the prayer was ended and reached for the dish Emma had put on the table. "Meat loaf and boiled turnips. My favorite. I hope you like them, Luke."

Emma stifled a small grin. Luke didn't like meat loaf, and he hated turnips.

"I do. It's one of my favorite meals, too," Luke said.

Her glance flew to his face. He was grinning at her with a twinkle in his eye. "I'm surprised that you remembered, Emma."

Of course he would find a way to put her on the spot. He knew exactly what she had done, but she could hardly claim she remembered he disliked them. She raised her chin a notch. "I didn't. It was a pure coincidence."

"A happy one for me, it seems." He loaded his plate and passed the platter to Roy.

Emma fumed silently as the meal continued, but a covert glance at Luke proved he hadn't touched his turnips and was only picking at his meat loaf. She took pity on him and fetched the half dozen leftover dinner rolls from the day before. She offered him the plate and he took three.

"What do you think of my collection, Luke?" her father asked.

"You have a good amount of salvageable equipment. It's going to take some time to get the bulk of it in running order."

"How much time do you reckon?"

"Six months, maybe. Truthfully, it would be better to wait until warmer weather to work on it."

"I reckon you're right about that." Disappointment clouded her father's expression.

"I think you should concentrate on getting your hardware store finished," Luke added quickly. "A lot of the small things like the horseshoes and nails can be sold in your store without waiting for a farm sale. The chain saws and handsaws will likely sell, too. This time of year, everyone needs firewood. Does the log splitter work?"

Roy shook his head. "We've been splitting our wood by hand for the past two years."

"That's too bad, but once your store is enclosed

and can be heated, repairing things like the log splitter and other small equipment will be much easier."

"That will be our plan, then," Zachariah announced. "Starting this afternoon, we'll get busy finishing the walls."

Luke buttered his roll. "Where did the solar panels in the hayloft come from?"

Zachariah scratched his chin. "Let me think. I remember now. I traded a green-broke horse to an *Englisch* fella over by Berlin. It was a poor trade on my part. I thought I could resell them for more, but most folks want them installed and guaranteed. I intended to read up on it but never got around to it. I still have that book somewhere."

"If you find it, I'd like to see it."

Her father looked her way. "Any idea where it might be, Emma?"

"It's in the bookcase in the living room where I put all the books you intend to read and never do." She smiled tenderly at him. He was a fine man, but he wasn't without his faults.

He chuckled and pointed his fork at Luke. "My daughter keeps me in line. A good thing it is, too. Her mother was just the same. Never settle for a woman that always lets you have your way, Luke."

"I won't," Luke said quietly. His gaze was fixed on her face.

She looked away first. The sound of the buggy outside caught her attention. She glanced past her father and saw Wayne drive in. He stepped down from his buggy, brushed off his coat and adjusted his hat before approaching the house.

Her dad glanced over his shoulder. "Well, it seems that Wayne isn't wasting any time."

"What does that mean?" Roy asked, looking perplexed.

Her father chuckled. "Nothing. I shall go see what he wants. Perhaps he can join us for our midday meal."

Emma closed her eyes and prayed that would not be the case. The thought of Luke watching Wayne court her was almost more than she could bear.

Her prayer went unanswered. Her father came in with Wayne behind him. "Set another place, Emma. Wayne will be joining us."

"This should be interesting." Luke watched her with a smirk twitching at the corner of his lips. "Wayne Hochstetler? I never would have guessed."

"Oh, be quiet and eat your turnips!" She pushed back from the table and went to fetch another plate.

There was nothing wrong with Wayne's appearance, Emma decided as he shed his coat and hat and took a seat beside Luke. The widower was a fine-looking man with thick black hair and a well-kept beard. He was tall with an athletic figure, but he didn't smile much.

Emma was hard-pressed to make the meal stretch to include another healthy appetite, but she was required by her faith to feed any person who came to her table. Luke offered Wayne some of his untouched turnips, and he accepted them with barely a nod. Emma passed the meat loaf to Wayne without taking any herself. She added a day-old roll to her plate instead. Cutting it in half, she buttered the crown. The meal progressed in silence, made all the more uncomfortable by her father's contented smile. She reached for the honey.

Luke caught her eye, gave her a wink and a nod as if signaling his approval. She wanted to pour the honey over his head, but restricted herself to adding it to her day-old roll.

When the meal was done, the men retired to the living room, leaving her alone at last. She hurried through the dishes so she could join them. Thankfully, her father was hard of hearing and she had no trouble listening to the conversation taking place in the other room.

"What brings you out this way?" Zachariah asked.

"I heard about Roy falling through the ice. I came to see how he was faring after his accident. I had a cousin who perished from pneumonia after a winter dunking. I hope you have seen the error of your ways, Roy. The *Englisch* machines are dangerous and only draw us into peril."

"I did learn not to take one out on the river ice. I'll stick to the snow-covered fields in the future."

Emma flinched at Roy's flippant tone.

"You jest with me, but your accident was not a laughing matter. The bishop may well be out to speak with your father about your attitude if it does not change soon."

"I have taken my son to task. He'll not repeat his mistake. I'm sure you have work waiting for you, Roy," her father said sharply. He wasn't pleased with Roy's attitude, either.

"We do," Luke said, and rose to leave.

Emma watched Roy saunter through the kitchen. She dried her hands on a towel and beckoned him with one finger. When he was close enough, she hissed, "Are you trying to embarrass our father?"

Roy glared over his shoulder. "What business does Wayne Hochstetler have threatening to send the bishop out here? We aren't members of his church. Why would our bishop care if I ride a snowmobile? I'm not baptized. I've done nothing wrong."

"It is the business of all good men who see others going astray to set the wrongdoer on a better path. Search your heart for *gelassenheit*, Roy."

"I don't want to be humble before Wayne."

"It's not about Wayne. *Gelassenheit* means yielding oneself to a higher authority. It means giving ourselves up to the church. Self-surrender, submission, yielding to the will of God and to others. It brings contentment and a calm spirit to our lives."

"Not to me." He shouldered past Luke, snatched his hat and coat from the pegs by the door, and stormed out.

Luke stepped close to her. "He's having a hard time about something, Emma. He'll come around."

"I hope so."

"I'll talk to him."

He was the last person she should turn to for help. "I'm more afraid of your advice than of leaving him alone."

He flinched slightly, and she was sorry she had been so abrupt. She clasped her hands in front of her and looked down. "Forgive me."

"There's nothing to forgive. Go in and enjoy your visitor."

"What makes you think Roy is having a hard time?" She glanced up to read the concern in his face.

"He mentioned a boy named Micah Yoder, a friend of his. I got the impression they don't see each other anymore."

"Micah was a member of Wayne's church. He

died almost a year ago. It will be exactly a year on Roy's birthday later this month."

"I do remember hearing about it. Some kind of farming accident, wasn't it? It must have been tough on Roy to lose a friend so young."

She gazed into his blue eyes. "It's hard to lose a friend no matter what age we are."

Luke knew Emma was referring to him. "I hurt a lot of people when I left home. I regret that, and I regret that you were one of them."

"It was a long time ago."

It felt like only yesterday. Should he try and make her understand why he left? Or was it best to leave it alone and move forward.

Her father called from the other room, "Emma, could you put on a pot of coffee?"

"Right away, *Daed*," she answered.

"Is Wayne the one?"

Luke thought she would deny it, but she didn't. "I'm considering him. He has a lot going for him."

"Such as?"

"He owns a nice farm. He has a five-year-old daughter who needs a mother. My *daed* and his are close friends. It would make my father happy."

"Will he make you happy?"

"He's reliable, Luke. That's important. He's a good man and a staunch member of the faithful."

"If he's the one, I'm glad. I want you to be happy."

She hardened her heart against his charm and the way his soft voice pulled at her heartstrings. "I gave you the chance to make me happy once, and you threw it back in my face. You have no say in my life now."

A muscle twitched in his jaw. "You're right. It's none of my business." He walked out the door without another word.

She watched him go and wished he had been more concerned about her happiness when it *was* his business.

Chapter Six

Luke chose to walk to his destination the next morning. It was cold, but the sky was cloudless and the rising sun promised a mild day. His boots crunched through the snow as he crossed the lawn to the edge of the roadway. Yesterday's warm temperatures had caused a minor thaw, but a thick crust had frozen over again during the night. He was almost at the covered bridge when he heard a shout behind him.

"*Onkel* Luke, wait for me."

He stopped and turned around. His six-year-old niece Hannah came hurrying toward him. She was light enough that she ran over the surface of the snow without breaking through. Her ever-present shadow, a yellow Lab named Bella, trotted at her heels.

Luke waited until she was closer. "What's new, buttercup?"

Hannah took his hand and settled into a walk

beside him. "We're going to practice our parts for the school Christmas pageant today. I already know my poem by heart. Do you want to hear it?"

"Sure."

Hannah stopped and folded her hands in front of her. In a loud clear voice, she recited her lines. She only stumbled once. When she was finished, she gave him a sad look. "That wasn't very good."

"It was fine. All you need is a little more practice."

"*Onkel* Timothy has been helping me. *Mamm* and *Grossmammi*, too."

Joshua had moved his wife, Mary, and her grandmother, Ada Kauffman, into a small house near the Bowman farm. "Timothy has been helping you? Is he any good at poetry?"

"I think he just comes over for *Grossmammi* Ada's gingerbread cookies."

"That sounds like Timothy."

"He's going to clean out our stable at school and help make the decorations for our program."

"Now that *doesn't* sound like Timothy." They crossed the river using the pedestrian walkway built along the side of the covered bridge. A horse and buggy trotted through on the road. Hannah waved to Jonas Beachy, the bishop, and his wife, Ellie. They both waved back.

Hannah glanced up at Luke. "Are you coming to visit our school?"

"I'm passing by, but I can't stay. I've got to see Jim Morgan and then I'm going to Zachariah Swartzentruber's place."

"I like Alvin Swartzentruber." She covered her mouth with her mittened hands and giggled.

Luke grinned. She was just too cute. "Does Alvin know that?"

She nodded, making the ties of her cap jiggle on her shoulders. "I told him."

"And does he like you?"

Her lower lip stuck out in a pout. "*Nee*, he likes Betty Lapp. She's in the seventh grade."

"I'm sorry."

She wrinkled her nose. "It's okay. Billy Lapp likes me."

"Is he related to Betty?"

"Her little brother. He's in the first grade with me. Our school is going to go caroling on second Christmas."

"Are you? That sounds like fun." Second Christmas, December 26, was a day normally devoted to visiting between Amish families and friends. Caroling was just one way they shared the joy of the season.

"We're going to a nursing home and a hospital. *Aenti* Rebecca and your *mamm* are holding a cookie exchange on December 20. I'm to invite all my friends. You can invite your friends, too.

I love Christmas, don't you? Are you coming to our school pageant on Christmas Eve?"

"I wouldn't miss it for anything."

"Alvin is going to sing a solo. He has a beautiful voice, only I'm not supposed to tell him that. Teacher Lillian says he mustn't get a *gross feelich*."

A "big feeling" was another way of saying pride. "I'm sure Alvin knows his singing gift comes from God."

"He does. I'm going to be one of the angels that appear to the shepherds. Teacher Lillian has decided our program will be all about the shepherds and the good news they heard first."

"Sounds like it will be a mighty *goot* program."

"*Onkel* Timothy is coming, too. He likes my teacher."

That was news, although Luke wasn't sure his source was reliable. He'd definitely ask Timothy about it soon. "I don't remember there being so much romance at Rider Hill School when I went there."

"What's romance?"

"Something for you to ask your mother about when you're eighteen."

"Will you be a hundred then?"

He chuckled. "I'm sure it will feel that way."

"Papa Nick and *Mammi* Miriam are coming to visit us. *Mamm* has been missing them something awful on account of she gets sick every morning."

Nick and Miriam Bradley were Hannah's mother's adoptive parents. Luke knew Nick well. He was the sheriff of Holmes County.

"I'm sorry to hear your mother isn't feeling well."

"Do you know when I told *Mammi* Anna about it, she just clapped her hands and laughed. I don't think that was very nice."

"My mother gets excited when she learns... company is coming." Luke chuckled, refusing to be drawn into the conversation on what morning sickness indicated.

By this time, they had reached the one-room schoolhouse set back from the road in a clearing. A young woman was standing on the step with a bell in her hand. Lillian Keim wore the typical Amish *kapp* and a long green dress beneath her coat and apron. Around her, a dozen children of all ages were walking in quietly. Hannah darted away, but stopped and turned to wave. "Bye, *Onkel* Luke."

"Study hard, Hannah."

"I will. Come on Bella. My teacher says Bella is the best scholar she's ever had."

The child and the dog loped toward the building. Bella would spend the day on the front steps of the school until the children came out for recess. When they went back to class, Bella would wait there until school was out and follow Hannah home. She wouldn't leave without her girl.

Hannah took Bella to her rug and stayed at her side after the others went in. The teacher went inside just as Alvin came tearing down the road. He jumped the split-rail fence at the edge of the school yard and hurried to the door. Hannah hopped up from her place beside Bella and stood squarely in front of him, blocking the doorway.

She smiled brightly. "*Guder mariye*, Alvin."

"Good morning, squirt. Morning, Bella." He stopped to pet the dog.

Hannah smiled shyly. "You sure can jump high. My aunt is having a cookie exchange party, and you're invited," she finished in a rush.

"*Danki*. We better go in. We're gonna be late." He slipped past her.

She sighed and followed him with a look of bliss on her face. Luke smiled. He would definitely have to warn Joshua that she was going to be a heartbreaker. A lot like another young woman who had attended school there. A woman he wouldn't stop thinking about even today. His heart grew light at the thought of seeing her soon, but he had something else to take care of first.

A quarter mile past the school, he turned into the snow-covered drive that led to Jim Morgan's place. Luke heard the engine of the snowmobile. He followed the sound to the pasture where Jim and Brian were unloading bales of hay from a small sled behind the machine and breaking them open for a group of hungry steers. Luke stayed by the gate until the brothers were finished. He opened it so they could drive through and then he closed it behind them.

"Thanks, Luke." Jim stepped off his machine. Brian stayed on the seat.

Luke gestured toward the snowmobile. "I'm glad to see you got her running."

Jim smiled. "It just took a little love."

"And some new spark plugs," Brian added.

"Which is coming out of your allowance. Are we still on for Friday?" Jim pulled off his gloves.

"That's what I wanted to ask you about." On even months, Luke had to report in with his parole officer at the agency in the city. It was a two-and-a-half-hour trip by car. Too far for a horse and buggy. On odd months, Officer Merlin came to Luke's home to check on his progress.

Jim pulled the pin holding the sled to the back of his snowmobile. When he had it free, he moved the sled to the side. "You don't have to ask. You know I'll always drive you."

"It's a big imposition. I hate to take advantage of you. I can call Sheriff Bradley. He'll take me if you're busy."

"I enjoy the trip."

"Can I go with you this time? I don't have school on Friday. It's in-service day for the teachers." Brian looked hopeful.

Jim considered it and nodded. "Okay. We can get some Christmas shopping done while we're in the city. Now, get going or you'll be late for school."

"Can I take the snowmobile?"

"I guess."

"Great! Thanks, bro." Brian slipped into the driver's seat and gunned the engine before tearing out of the yard and down the lane.

"He's growing up fast." Luke watched him until he rounded a curve and was lost from sight.

"Just as fast as we did. You're almost finished with your sentence. That has to feel good."

"It does. Two more visits with my parole officer and then I'm a free man."

"This Friday and then when is your last visit?"

"The day before Christmas."

"Is he coming here?"

Luke shook his head. "I'll have to go into the office for my final visit, too." Then the English law said his debt to society had been paid in full. Maybe when that day came, he would be free of the guilt he carried in his heart like a weighty stone.

"What will you do then?"

Luke knew what Jim was asking. Was he going to remain Amish or was he going back into the world. "I don't know. I never really fit in here."

"Yes, you did. You didn't want to believe that,

but I could see it. I'm sorry I got you into so much trouble. I didn't have my head on straight after my parents were killed. Doing drugs was stupid, but I couldn't face the responsibility of raising Brian. I tried to party myself into oblivion. I didn't mean to drag you down with me. I never should have offered that stuff to you."

"I made my own choices, Jim. I didn't have my head on straight, either. I got hooked, and you got your act together."

"Do you ever think about using again?"

"Every day. Thankfully, there's not much drug traffic in Bowmans Crossing."

"Luke, if you wanted to use again, you'd find a way, even in Bowmans Crossing. You're stronger than you know."

"Am I? I'm not so sure. How do you stay clean?"

"I think about what I stand to lose. The day we got busted together was the day I saw the light, Luke."

"I remember. We were coming back from a party and we got pulled over for a busted headlight."

"With a pound of marijuana in a backpack on the backseat. Man, I was so stupid."

"We both were."

"You told the cops that the drugs were yours when they were mine so they let me go. I watched them cart you off to jail, and I knew if it had been me, there wouldn't be anyone to take care of my brother. I owe you plenty for that."

It had been Luke's first arrest. He'd spent two nights in jail before his father paid his bail. Jim had helped Luke's father hire a lawyer. The lawyer got Luke released on probation because it was his first offense, but Luke had been too ashamed to go home. Instead, he had Jim take him to the bus station.

"You've more than made up for it these past months." If Luke had someone to love and care for like Jim did with his younger brother, would he be strong enough to withstand temptation, too? Maybe.

"Hope so. I heard Zachariah Swartzentruber might be opening a hardware store. Is that true?"

"It is. I'm helping him get ready. He wants to open the Monday after Christmas."

"This area could use one that doesn't gouge prices like the one the other side of Berlin does, but I'm afraid I can't see Zachariah successfully running a business. Now, Emma—that would be a different story."

"How so?"

"She knows how to drive a bargain. She buys a side of beef from me every year, and I end up almost giving it to her. Lots of the non-Amish I know get their eggs and vegetables from her. She's well-known for fair dealing. Her dad's well-known for collecting junk."

Luke chuckled. "That he is. Emma always had a good head on her shoulders." Except for the night she tried to run away with him. That night he had been the responsible one—for the first time in his life.

"You and Emma were an item at one time. I see that flame has been rekindled."

"*Nee*, what makes you say that?" He denied it to his friend, but he couldn't deny it to himself.

"The way your eyes light up when you say her name. You can't fool me. I see the signs. Does she feel the same?"

Luke shook his head. "She can barely stand the sight of me."

"Maybe that was the reason she was always asking about you when you were in jail."

"Emma asked about me?" Luke couldn't believe that.

"Every time I stopped in to get eggs, she wanted to know if I had heard from you. If you were doing okay. Three measly letters from you was all I had to share, but she never stopped asking until the day you got out."

"That doesn't make any sense." Why had Emma begged news from Jim and not from Luke's parents? Then the answer occurred to him. She had been ashamed of her relationship with him and didn't want members of her church to know she had been dating a drug user.

Still, that she had asked about him at all meant

she had continued to care about him. She hadn't gone on with her life and forgotten about him as he told her to do.

Did any of those feelings for him remain?

Emma discovered she didn't need to worry about Luke being under foot while he was working for her father. By his second day on the job, he had perfected the art of staying out of her way. Roy was the one who told her Luke would be bringing his lunches and not to plan on feeding him. If her unappetizing meal hadn't driven him from her table, her sharp tongue had. It should have made her happy, but it didn't.

By late afternoon, she couldn't stand it any longer. When she heard a lull in the hammering, she opened the door that led from the porch to the new store.

She paused in surprise. Luke had gotten a lot done. The walls of the store were up and insulation was pressed into the spaces between the studs. A coal stove sat glowing red in the center of the room, its chimney already in place. Sheetrock panels sat at the rear of the room waiting to go up on the ceiling. A large bay window at the front allowed in plenty of natural light and would make the perfect place to showcase the goods her father planned to sell. Maybe some of the gourd birdhouses that Luke painted could hang there. It was truly beginning to look like a store. Maybe this idea of her father's was a good one, after all.

Zachariah looked up from measuring a plank. "Emma, come see what we've gotten done. Luke is a hard taskmaster."

She glanced at Roy. He shook his head. At least her father wasn't being allowed to overdo it. He looked a bit better today. There was a sparkle in his eyes that had been missing for a while.

Luke was strapping on a pair of drywall stilts. He nodded to acknowledge her, but didn't pause. When he was ready, Roy lifted one end of the sheet and Luke grabbed the other. Using crosspieces on long poles, they wedged the sheet into position. Luke secured it with screws using a battery-operated drill. Outside, her father's gasoline generator hummed away as it supplied the electricity for a bank of lights and a battery-charging station.

"What do you think?" her father asked.

She thought Luke's muscular shoulders and arms were showing to advantage as they bulged beneath the fabric of his blue shirt, but she didn't say that. Instead, she turned to her father. "It looks like you're getting a lot done. You are taking it easy, aren't you? You know the doctor said you should."

He scowled at her. "Don't fuss. I'm fine. Luke and Roy aren't letting me lift anything heavier than a pencil."

When Luke finished fastening the sheet, he turned toward her. "Measure twice, cut once. Making sure the measurements are accurate is the most important part of the job, Zachariah. If the walls are as crooked as a dog's hind leg, it will be your fault."

She folded her arms together. "They look straight to me. Can I help?"

Luke lifted the next sheet of drywall. "We're almost done for the day."

Her father patted her shoulder. "Some *kaffi* would be *wunderbar.*"

"I can manage that easy enough." She left the room feeling better about her father's project. Luke seemed to know what he was doing.

She returned fifteen minutes later with four mugs of coffee on a tray. The warm, pungent aroma mixed with the smell of sawdust and plaster.

"*Danki*, child." Her father took a cup and sat on a sawhorse.

Roy took his and squatted nearby. Luke accepted a cup, walked away to the other side of the room and leaned against the wall still on his stilts. He was making it clear that he could avoid her. It was what she wanted, wasn't it? So why did it hurt to be ignored?

"What's next after this?" Emma surveyed the space.

"I'm not rightly sure." Her father glanced around, seemingly at a loss.

"We'll start building the shelves," Roy said. "Luke suggested we put the counters on casters so we can move them aside and hold church services in here."

"There is plenty of space for that." More space than her living room and kitchen combined. The walls in the downstairs part of the house could be moved back to open the area for services. She usually only had to ready the place once or twice a year. The cleaning and preparation was a major undertaking. Everyone in the congregation took their turn at hosting the meeting so that no one family had the burden.

Her father rose. "Roy, where did I put that box of casters?"

"Beats me, *Daed*."

"I think I put them in the barn, or maybe on the back porch."

Roy took another sip and then put his half-empty mug on Emma's tray. "I'll help you look for them."

The two men went out, leaving Emma waiting in awkward silence for Luke to finish his drink. She wound the ribbon of her *kapp* around her finger and tried to look anywhere but at him.

"You make *goot* coffee."

"Danki." She picked up her mug to give her hands something to do.

"What's your secret?"

She scowled at him. "I don't know what you mean."

"What's your secret to such good coffee?"

Of course he wasn't talking about her father's illness. She relaxed and took a sip. "I buy the expensive brand and I only use spring water. That and I add a teaspoon of sugar to the grounds."

He sat on the sawhorse and unbuckled his stilts. "I knew something was different about yours. *Mamm* makes good coffee but yours is better. I'm not trying to give you a *gross feelich*."

"*Nee*, you wouldn't want to do that." He would never want to make her feel special because she wasn't special to him.

He laid the stilts aside. "I have an invitation from Hannah. Rebecca and *Mamm* are having a cookie exchange on December 20, and I was told I could invite my friends."

His words triggered a surge of warmth in her midsection. Wouldn't it be nice if they could be friends again?

"*Danki*, cookie exchanges are always fun. Tell, Hannah, Rebecca and your mother I can make it."

"*Goot.*" He looked around. "What are your father's plans for this place when we get it done?"

The business was a safer subject. "I'm not sure. Will it be ready to open by the week after Christmas?"

"Even if we work night and day, I doubt we'll have it done by then."

"He has dreamed about having a hardware store for years, but until recently, he hasn't found the time to actually open it. He wants a business Roy can grow into."

"I hope it works out for him, and for you. And right on cue, here comes Wayne." He gestured toward the window and she saw Wayne getting out of his buggy. He paused and surveyed the outside of the building.

Luke came toward her and put his mug on her tray. "I'll leave you two alone. I'm sure he hasn't come to see me."

Emma realized with a start that she didn't want to be left alone with Wayne. She started to set the tray aside, but a half-empty mug tipped over and spilled on her white apron. She hissed in displeasure, whipped it off, rolled it into a bundle and tossed it onto a box on the window seat. "There's no need to run away."

Luke glanced at her sharply. "Then I'll start taping the drywall joints. The sooner we get them done, the sooner we can get some paint on the walls. Have you chosen a color?"

Wayne came through the plastic sheet that was covering the doorway. "Good day."

Emma smiled at him. "Good day, Wayne. What can I help you with?"

"I just stopped by to see the progress. After

seeing the half-finished shell sitting here for years, it's quite a change to see the walls up."

"I wonder what paint color would look good. What do you think?" she asked.

Wayne glanced around. "Gray or green would look businesslike."

She nodded. "It would have to be a pale gray or a nice mint green to keep the place bright on cloudy days."

"A few well-placed ceiling lights will do that. It's a shame I don't know more about the solar panels your father has. Lighting without the cost of propane or oil would be an advantage," Luke said.

Wayne crossed his arms. "A man only needs the light of the sun to work by. God provides all we need. Such technology is not fitting for us. We must remain apart from the world."

"Using solar power is using God's power grid. Some Amish communities have already embraced it," Luke said.

Wayne scowled deeply at him. "And many have not."

The two men glared at each other. Luke glanced at her, and his face softened. "I should be getting home. It was nice chatting with you, Wayne. Get Emma to fix you a cup of coffee. You'll enjoy it. See you tomorrow, Emma."

She watched him leave and couldn't help comparing the two men. Luke was much better looking, but looks weren't everything. Hadn't she learned that lesson? A handsome face could hide an insincere heart. A steady, reliable, devout man was much more desirable in a mate. If only Wayne's smile set her pulse racing the way Luke's did.

The problem wasn't with Wayne. It was with her.

He took his hat off and swept a hand through his hair. "I hope this isn't a bad time."

"For what?" She resisted the urge to flee the room.

"Your father has made it known that I am welcome to come courting you. I would know your feelings on the subject."

How should she answer him?

Chapter Seven

Emma rearranged the mugs on her platter, playing for time to find the right answer. "Courting is a very serious undertaking, Wayne."

He nodded. "I agree. We have no need to rush into anything."

"I've not met your daughter. I feel that is important before I give you an answer. She may not like me."

"A point well taken, although the child's feelings on the subject will not sway mine."

Emma looked him full in the face. "Her feelings matter."

"Sophie is an obedient child."

Emma glanced away. "I was not suggesting otherwise."

"She will accept you."

"My cousin Rebecca Bowman is hosting a cookie exchange with her mother-in-law at Anna Bowman's home in two weeks. If you agree to it, I will take Sophie with me and we can get to know each other."

"I'm not sure that is a good idea."

That stumped her. "Why not?"

"The Bowmans are not members of my church."

"Neither am I."

"I'm sure Isaac and Anna are good people, but two of their sons have brought shame on the family."

Emma plopped her tray down and fisted her hands on her hips. "And those sons have repented and been forgiven by the family and by their church. Are you holding yourself above their bishop's ruling?"

"*Nee*, but a man must take care that his children are not exposed to worldly things. Luke Bowman is not yet baptized, nor are his brothers Noah and Timothy. I have seen Noah using a cell phone, and I have seen Luke driving a car."

The fact that Luke was still driving shocked her. She struggled not to let it show on her face. "I hope you will trust me not to let your daughter ride in a car with him."

He seemed taken aback by her displeasure. "Of course. If I did not trust you, I would not be considering courting you. You are known to all as a modest and worthy woman."

"I am happy to hear that."

"You may take Sophie to the cookie exchange if you like."

She picked up her tray again. "Please tell your daughter that I'm looking forward to meeting her. Now, I must get over to the school. I promised Lillian Keim that I would help her with the children's costumes for the Christmas play. Good day."

Luke had never been more tempted to listen at the keyhole in his entire life. He wanted to know how serious Emma was about Wayne. How serious Wayne was about her. Did he love her? Did she love him? The thought brought a sick feeling to Luke's stomach.

Instead of eavesdropping, Luke had forced his feet to head for home. Emma's relationship with Wayne was none of his business.

Telling himself that and actually accepting the fact were two different sides of the same coin. No matter how many times he tried, he couldn't bear the idea of the two of them together. Luke knew Emma would make up her own mind and he had no say in that. Once he might have, but not anymore.

Before long, he approached the school yard. Two new snowmen stood waving their twig arms at passersby. The bright sunshine had melted the snow into perfect snowball-making conditions and it was clear the schoolchildren had taken advantage of it during their recess.

Luke scooped up a handful and packed it into a ball. He took aim at the nearest snowman, imagining it was Wayne and let fly. He missed.

He made a second snowball and tried again. He went wider this time.

Great. He couldn't best an imaginary version of Wayne. How could he hope to best the real man? Certainly not with a snowball.

"You're out of practice."

Luke looked down the road and saw Timothy approaching. Scooping up a handful of snow again, Luke grinned at his brother. "Maybe I'm better with a moving target."

He fired and the snowball splattered against Timothy's dark coat. Feeling vindicated, Luke kept walking toward his brother. He wasn't surprised when Timothy nailed him with a snowball in return. He deserved it.

Dusting the crystals from his coat, Luke waited until Timothy was beside him. His brother brushed at his own coat. "As much as I would enjoy a full-scale war with you, I'm already late for my appointment."

"Your appointment with the pretty schoolteacher?" To Luke's surprise, Timothy blushed. So he did like Teacher Lillian.

"I volunteered to help with the Christmas pageant sets and clean the stable. That's all."

Luke winked at him. "That is very community-minded of you."

"The school can use more help. What are you doing this evening?"

What was he doing? Nothing but moping over Emma's relationship with Wayne. Working with schoolkids wasn't Luke's thing, but he could happily give his brother a hand. "Unless there is work waiting for me at home, I'm free. I could help you."

"Samuel has everything in hand at home."

"*Goot.* What kind of set are we building? Hannah said the program would be about the shepherds."

"I notice you didn't volunteer for stable work."

"You're much more suited to that job. I have an artistic flair."

"I'm not sure what Lillian has planned, but whatever it is, I'll build it for her."

Timothy was the middle brother. Luke and Samuel were older. Joshua and Noah were both younger. Timothy was the easygoing one. He liked helping people. He had a knack for fixing machinery that rivaled Luke's and a winning way with customers. Luke was glad if his little brother had found a woman to make him happy.

The school doors opened and the scholars came walking out. They stayed in orderly two-by-two formations until they reached the bottom of the steps. Then they rushed across the school grounds. Some headed for home on foot while others waited to be picked up by the line of buggies approaching on the roadway. Snowballs began flying almost immediately followed by shrieks and shouts.

Hannah was among the last to come out. Bella got up from her rug, raced down the steps and frolicked beside the child in the snow. A number of children stopped to give her a goodbye pat before heading off. Hannah waved to Timothy and Luke, but walked on with another girl about her own age.

Lillian Keim stood on the top step waiting as Luke and Timothy approached. She kept her gaze down as befit a demure Amish maiden. "I want to thank you again for your offer of help, Timothy. The children deeply appreciate it."

Luke couldn't detect a hint of her feelings about his brother in her manner or her words.

Timothy said, "I hope you don't mind that I have brought Luke to help."

"Not at all. Come in. A few of the eighth-grade children are staying over to help as well."

Luke followed the teacher and Timothy into the building. It was the same school all the Bowman brothers had attended. Inside, it was as if nothing had changed except for the art posters drawn by childish hands that adorned a strip of corkboard above the blackboard. Luke fondly remembered the prize he had won for the best drawing of a horse in the second grade.

The same oversize desk sat on a raised platform at the front. Even the teacher's chair was the same one Luke remembered. He had loosened the wheels on it so that when his teacher sat down it teetered precariously, scaring the woman half to death. He'd had to write an apology one hundred times on the blackboard while the other kids were outside playing ball. As painful as that was, it paled in comparison to his father's stern punishment that night. He wondered if any of Lillian's scholars had pulled such pranks on her and decided they had. Boys were boys, after all.

The student desks were arranged from smallest to adult-size in rows either side of a wide center aisle. The plain oak planks of the floor were scuffed and scratched, but swept clean, a task assigned to the oldest girls in turn. The tall windows on each side of the single room let in plenty of light. Only the squat black coal stove was missing from its place near the front of the room. He turned to Timothy. "They got rid of that stove after I had to carry a ton of coal in when I was here?"

"The school board decided putting a new propane furnace in the basement was a better investment than buying and storing coal."

It was toasty warm in the building. "I wish they had come to that conclusion before I left school."

He saw Alvin with two other boys standing on one side of the teacher's desk while four young girls stood on the other side. The girls were busy exchanging ideas about the program. The boys were busy trying not to look bored.

Lillian addressed the group. "We are waiting on one more volunteer to get this planning meeting started. I want to thank everyone for staying after to help."

The outside door opened. Luke turned to see Emma rush in. "I'm sorry I'm late."

She came to a dead stop when she caught sight of him.

What was Luke doing here?

Emma sought Lillian's gaze and arched an eyebrow in query. Lillian shrugged, looking sorry for the situation.

She said, "You aren't late. Now that you are here, we can get started."

Emma pulled off her cape and bonnet, laying them on one of the chairs. Lillian opened a sketchbook on her desk. "We are going to tell the Christmas story from the view of the shepherds tending their flocks."

"We can glue cotton balls to Alvin and make him a sheep," Abram Shetler suggested as he nudged Alvin. He was one of her brother's friends and in the same grade.

The other boy, Jacob Weaver, laughed and said, "Baa, baa."

The girls giggled. Alvin rolled his eyes but didn't say anything.

Lillian gave them a stern look, and they fell silent.

Emma came up to the desk. Luke took a step back, placing Timothy between them. She refused to look his way. "What kind of costumes do you have in mind?"

"Four shepherds, nine angels, Mary, Joseph and the innkeeper. Is that too much?"

Emma shook her head. "I'm sure some of the mothers will help with the sewing."

"What do you want for sets?" Timothy asked.

Lillian tentatively pushed her sketchbook toward him. "I thought of having the children paint two backdrops. One depicting the hills and sheep, and the other depicting the stable and inn in Bethlehem."

He studied her drawing. "You'll need some way to affix them to the wall and yet allow them to be changed easily." He looked at Luke. "What do you think? You're the artist in the family."

Emma had seen the brightly painted and decorated gourd birdhouses that Luke's mother sold in her gift shop. Luke did indeed have an artist's touch.

He rubbed his jaw as he studied Lillian's drawings. "I'd paint them on canvas and tack the canvas to a freestanding frame. Paper will tear too easily. Have the hills painted on one side, turn the frame around and have Bethlehem on the other side."

Lillian brightened and gave Luke a sweet smile. "That's a wonderful idea. That way, we could start the story at the inn, turn the panel and have the shepherd's part and then turn it back once more to the stable scene. How large could you make it? Could you design it so that it wouldn't tip over easily? Is it too worldly for an Amish school program?"

"I don't think so," Timothy said quickly. "Not if the children paint it. We could make it six feet high and six feet wide. Would that be large enough?"

Luke paced off the platform that held the desk and would serve as the stage for the children. "We've got fifteen feet to work with. Why not make two panels and have the backgrounds be twice as big. That way Bishop Beachy can see it without his eyeglasses."

They all chuckled. The bishop was well-known as a man who was forever leaving his glasses somewhere.

Lillian folded her sketchbook closed. "These are very good suggestions. I hope our production will be one of the best yet. The children and all their families look forward to this each year."

Emma knew that was true. It was the one time of year when Amish children were encouraged to perform. The programs she had participated in during her school years were among her fondest memories. She glanced at Luke. Did he recall the time he had played Joseph and she had played Mary when they were in the third grade? It had been the beginning of her crush on him. One that had never faded. Even to this day.

With blinding clarity, she knew it was true. He was and always would be her first love. That would never change.

Was she foolish to consider marrying someone else when Luke still held a place in her heart? Would it be fair to ask a husband to live in the shadow of another man?

Luke said he had changed, but she wasn't a naive teenager anymore. She would have to know with absolute certainty that he would remain Amish before she would consider letting him into her heart again. If he had any interest, and she hadn't seen a clear sign of that.

"What do you think, Emma?"

Jerked back to the present by Lillian's question, Emma flushed. "I'm sorry. I was daydreaming."

"I asked if you thought the children could paint such large pictures."

"If someone were to draw the lines and lay out what colors were to be used, I'm sure the children could follow the directions. You might want to give the younger ones the simpler parts to color."

Lillian looked at her girls. "Are you prepared to take this on?"

"*Ja*, Teacher. We can do it," they agreed together.

"Emma, would you be able to supervise them?"

"I'm afraid I'm going to have my hands full with our store and making costumes." As much as she wanted to help her friend, she knew her limits.

"I'll oversee the painting part of the project," Luke said. "Timothy and the boys can build the frames and make sure they are easy to move but hard to tip over."

Lillian pressed her lips together. Emma knew she was considering if it was proper to allow Luke, an unmarried man, to supervise the young women under her care.

Lillian looked at Emma. "If I can find someone else to make the costumes, will you help Luke and the girls with the painting?"

The young teacher's expression told Emma she was sorry for putting her in an awkward situation but she had little choice. Emma nodded in understanding. The program was important. "I can help paint."

Not only would she have to have Luke at the store every day until it was done, she'd have to see him in the evenings, too.

Lillian smiled wanly. *"Danki."*

Timothy turned to Luke. "Do you think Mary and *Mamm* would help with the costumes?"

Luke shrugged. "Mary likes to sew. We can ask. After all, Hannah told me she is going to be one of the angels, so Mary may already be expecting to make something."

Emma glanced at Luke. He was gazing at her intently. Why? What was he thinking?

"Mamm, what do you know about Wayne Hochstetler?"

Luke stayed behind in the kitchen after supper was finished that evening. His father and his brothers had all gone into the other room to discuss what would be needed in the business while Isaac and Anna were on vacation. Luke sat staring into the half-empty glass of milk in his hand. He had been given the opportunity to spend time working with Emma. He couldn't deny he liked the idea, but was it too little too late? How could he know?

His mother dried her hands on a towel. "About Wayne Hochstetler? Not much, really. He's a widower. His wife passed away two years ago after a brief illness. He has a five-year-old daughter.

His father is the bishop of their district. Why are you interested?"

"I ran into Wayne at Zachariah's again today."

"Wayne's father and Zachariah are neighbors, and they've always been close friends, although they belong to different church districts."

"I had the feeling he was there to see Emma."

"Really? I guess that's not surprising. She would make a good wife and a good mother for his daughter. She has had plenty of practice raising those brothers of hers."

"You think it would be a good match?"

"I couldn't say one way or the other. The important thing is if the *couple* believes it's a good match. It takes a lot of prayer to decide on a spouse. They must be sure it is the path chosen by God for them. Why this interest in Wayne?"

"No reason." He rolled the glass between his hands.

His mother chuckled. "Let me rephrase my question. Why this sudden interest in Emma's courtship?"

"I don't know that she is being courted." He propped his elbows on the table.

"I always thought you two would make a match of it."

He shook his head. "Emma is too good for me."

"So you are looking for a floozy."

He started laughing. "Do you even know what a floozy is?"

"A woman with a poor reputation that is well deserved. I was not born yesterday."

"And how many floozies do you know?"

"I shall leave you to wonder about that. Emma is not too good for you. You're mistaken about that. You have a kind heart, Luke, but you won't give up your crutch."

"What crutch is that?" He knew the answer but wondered if his mother did.

"Your guilt. You wield it like a club to beat away the goodness of others and to keep happiness from your door."

He thought his crutch was the drugs. He hadn't considered it was the guilt he carried. "I've done some bad things. Things I'm too ashamed to share with you or anyone."

"When you are baptized, Luke, every sin will be forgiven, even the ones I do not know about, for God *knows* all things and *forgives* all things if you allow Him. There is nothing you can keep hidden from our Lord. You would be surprised by the things you have not kept hidden from me. You cannot atone for your sins by denying yourself a chance to love and be loved by someone."

"So how do I atone for my sins?"

"Our Savior laid down His life on the cross for your sins, Luke. Why don't you think that is enough? Salvation is His gift to you. He asks only that you love Him and obey His commandments."

"How is it that I have such a wise mother?"

She smiled and winked at him. "Another gift from God. Cherish your gifts, Luke, and leave your mistakes in the past where they belong."

"I don't know if I can."

She reached out and knocked his glass over, sending milk spreading across the tabletop. "Put the milk back in your glass, Luke."

He backed away from the table to keep the milk from dripping in his lap. "*Mamm*, you know I can't do that."

She fisted her hands on her hips and glared at him. "*Nee*, you cannot. You can sit and moan about your empty glass or you can pour yourself another. What's done can't be undone, so stop complaining about it."

"Are you angry with me?"

"I am. You are wasting the gifts God has given you. Now get out of the kitchen so I can finish my dishes. If you want another glass of milk, get it yourself. If you want to go out with Emma, ask her. There's no guarantee you won't make a mess again, but at least you'll be going forward instead of sitting here crying over spilled milk."

"Asking Emma out isn't that easy."

"How do you know? Have you tried it?"

He raised both eyebrows. "Of course not. I told you I think Wayne may be courting her."

"But you don't know for sure."

The outside door opened. Samuel and Rebecca came in with their arms loaded with greenery. Rebecca's cheeks were rosy and flushed. "We've brought some pine boughs to decorate the window ledges and mantel. I love their fragrance at the holidays."

"I love the taste of sweets at the holidays." Samuel had a smug smile on his face that told Luke he'd been kissing his wife on their outing. She gave him a saucy grin as they went into the living room.

Luke's mother folded her arms and chuckled. "What you need is a go-between to discover Emma's feelings. I know just who to ask. Shall I?"

Chapter Eight

Luke mulled over his mother's words as he finished the rest of the drywall in Zachariah's shop the next morning. Maybe *Mamm* was right. Maybe he should give his relationship with Emma another try. The trouble was, he had no idea if she was in love with Wayne or not. The last thing he wanted was to jeopardize her future happiness.

An Amish fellow could ask a girl's friends, or a family member like her brother, if she would be willing to walk out with him. Luke couldn't imagine asking Roy, but his mother's idea about asking Rebecca to be his go-between wasn't a bad idea.

He hadn't spoken to his sister-in-law when he had the chance last night. He needed to work up to that conversation. Maybe after supper tonight if he could get her aside without Samuel knowing about it. Luke didn't relish the thought of all the brotherly ribbing he would get if any of his brothers found out he was asking Rebecca to be his go-between.

"Will you be eating lunch with us today?" Emma asked from behind him. He hadn't heard her come in. He spun around and a glop of dry-wall mud flew off his trowel. It landed on her black shoe. He stared at it in speechless shock.

This was not a good start.

He raised his eyes to her face. She was glaring at him, but there was a slight twitch at the corner of her mouth. "A simple no would suffice. If my cooking is that bad, just say so."

"It's not that. I'm sorry. Let me get something." He turned around looking for a rag, anything to clean her shoe. He spied a bundle of cloth on the window seat, snatched it up and began to wipe the mess off her foot. When he had most of it rubbed off, he stood with a sheepish grin. "There."

She held out her hand. "May I have my apron back now?"

"Your what?" He glanced at the gray-plaster-loaded cloth in his hand.

"My apron. I took it off in here yesterday and I was looking for it."

He held it out. "I'm sorry about that."

She took it between two fingers. "It will wash. As will my shoe. Are you eating with us today?"

"Am I restricted to bread and water?"

"If you don't make another mess, you might get a little gravy on your bread crumbs."

"*Danki.* I'll join you for the meal."

She glanced around. "*Goot.* Where is my father?"

"He's sorting through boxes in the barn, trying to see what we can sell. I think he hates to part with any of it."

"I know he wants this business for Roy. Is there any hope that it won't become a money pit?"

He shrugged. "*Daed* and Samuel have the business sense in the family. I break things and sometimes fix things. You can ask for their suggestions."

She bristled slightly. "I'm sure we'll manage."

He gestured with his trowel. "I'm sure you will. I need to get this mud on the walls before it dries."

"Lunch will be in half an hour."

"I appreciate it, and you're a *goot* cook. Has Wayne sampled your cherry cobbler?"

"I haven't cooked anything for him."

That was promising. "Your cherry cobbler and your gooseberry tarts, those were my favorites. Along with meat loaf and boiled turnips, of course."

She flushed a dull red. "I'll have to remember that."

He chuckled as she spun around and left the

room. He liked that he had flustered her. It meant she wasn't indifferent to him. He went back to work and began whistling a cheery Christmas tune. If she wasn't indifferent to him, he might have a chance. *If* he proceeded carefully.

Emma dropped her dirty apron in the sink and turned on the water to let it soak. She pulled a rag from a bottom drawer and moistened it beneath the faucet. Sitting down on a kitchen chair, she pulled off her shoe and chuckled. Luke's shocked expression was the funniest thing she had seen all week.

She sobered. He used to make her laugh all the time. His outrageous antics had horrified the elders in their church, but she knew he was just trying to get a rise out of people. Their teacher had called it attention-seeking behavior, and looking back, Emma saw the woman had been right.

But somewhere along the way, his pranks had turned from playful to serious and ultimately ruinous for him. And for her. As much as she wanted to believe he was a changed man, she just couldn't. She finished cleaning her shoe, put it on and went back to work. Her days of mooning over Luke Bowman were long gone. She had a house to run, and soon she would have a business to run, too.

The thought brought her up short. If the

business became even modestly successful, why would she have to marry to care for her brothers? Why couldn't she and Roy manage it together? She didn't know much about running a business, but she could learn. It might be a far-fetched plan considering the store wasn't even open, but it had definite appeal.

When the men came in to eat lunch, she had it all on the table for them. After silent prayer, she waited to speak until everyone had their food. "Have you enough items to get the store started, Papa, or will you need to buy more?"

"I don't know."

"Some of his things are so old, I doubt we'll be able to give them away." Roy helped himself to another biscuit.

"What kind of old things?" Emma passed him the jam she knew he liked.

"Sewing machines and old coal stoves."

"I wasn't picky about the junk I hauled home." Her father looked tired today. There was a droop to his shoulders and his cheeks were pale.

"The *Englisch* have a love of antiques. You could call it a hardware and antiques market. That might bring in more customers," Luke suggested.

"*Nee*, it will be Swartzentruber and Sons Hardware Store. Nuts and bolts and shoes for the horses. Things my Amish neighbors can use."

Emma folded her hands and rested her elbows

on the table. "I think Luke is right. I don't think you should limit yourself to just the Amish."

"We shall see how it goes. I want it to be ready by Christmas. How much still has to be done inside, Luke?"

"The mud needs to dry overnight. It really should cure for two days in this weather. After that, sanding and priming and then paint. A week should see it done. I'd say another two weeks to put in the shelves and counters and a week to stock and price things."

"That is too long. We must get it done sooner."

"Papa, what will it hurt to open a little later?" she asked gently. He was getting too upset.

Her father glared at her. "The longer it takes the less money we make."

"Have you given a thought to using solar power in your store?"

Emma gave Luke a grateful glance for his quick change of subject. "Why solar?"

Her father stroked his chin. "I've not given any thought to it. How would it benefit us?"

"I could charge my cell phone," Roy said with a grin.

Emma scowled at him and he resumed eating. "Other than the phone my brother is not supposed to have, why would we want to incur the expense of putting in solar?"

"You already own the panels. You'd only need someone to install them, so it would be almost free power for charging batteries and lighting for the store. The bishop approved the use of electricity in my father's woodworking shop. We use a diesel generator." He began eating again.

Her father smiled. "This might be a good idea, Luke. The bishop would have to approve my use of electricity as well. Since we can't paint tomorrow, I will go see him. You must come with me. You are familiar with this technology."

Luke paused with his fork halfway to his mouth. "I can't go with you tomorrow."

Her father's scowl returned. "Why not?"

Emma saw a guarded look settle over Luke's expression. "I have another appointment."

"He has to see his parole officer," Roy said.

Luke slowly lowered his fork to his plate as a deep red flush crept up his cheeks. "That's right."

"I thought that bad business was behind you." Emma hadn't forgotten about the time he served in prison, but he had been home for over a year.

"I received an early release, but I'm on parole until I've served my entire sentence. I have to meet with my parole officer once a month until then."

"What happens if you don't?" Emma asked.

Luke stared at his plate, not meeting her gaze. "If I violate the terms of my parole, I can be sent back to prison to finish serving my time there plus whatever additional time they decide to tack on for my failure to follow the rules."

He pushed away from the table. "Zachariah, I'll start putting together some of those shelves. I can paint them while I'm waiting on the mud to dry."

He left the room with a good portion of his meal still on his plate. Emma turned to Roy. "How did you know about Luke's parole meeting?"

"Luke talked about being in prison the other day. I saw Brian Morgan yesterday, and he mentioned he was going into the city with Jim and Luke on Friday. I asked if it was for Luke's parole meeting. Brian looked surprised and said he wasn't supposed to talk about it, but I told him I already knew."

"You were gossiping about Luke? I'm ashamed of you."

"It's not gossip if it's true, and Brian already knew, anyway."

"Father, did you know about this?"

"*Nee*, I did not, but I don't see what difference it makes. The *Englisch* law is none of our business."

It shouldn't make a difference, but it did. It was a harsh reminder that Luke had been more than a wild and unreliable youth. He had fallen far from his faith and turned a deaf ear to the pleas of his family to reconcile until he had been released from prison. He claimed he had changed. It seemed as if he had, but how could she be sure?

Then she realized that she couldn't. She had to accept Luke's word.

This was a test of her faith. Could she live her beliefs?

Recalling the look of shame on Luke's face brought shame to her, too. He didn't deserve to have his past mistakes displayed before all of them. "Roy, you must never mention this again, not even to Alvin. What is forgiven is over. It should never be spoken about. Do you understand?"

"I guess." He shifted uncomfortably in his seat.

She rose from the table. "I will apologize for you. Luke needs to know we will not hold his past against him. It is wrong to do so."

Roy held up his hands. "I don't hold it against him."

"Nor do I," her father stated.

"Then I alone have been guilty of that sin. Clear the table for me, please, Roy. I'll be back shortly."

Luke hammered in the nail with much more force than necessary. Each beat of the hammer shouted, *Fool! Fool! Fool!*

He'd seen the shock on Emma's face. Now that she knew he was still on parole, she would have even less to do with him. Like the rest of the community, she had assumed his past was behind him. Now it stood like a wall between them because he'd lacked the courage to tell her about it. He had lied by omission. Any trust that had developed between them was surely gone.

He pulled a second board in place and drove in another nail with such force that it split the wood. He pried out the nail and threw the piece aside in disgust.

"Luke, may I speak with you?"

The sound of her soft voice behind him brought him up short. He didn't look at her. "I should have told your father about my parole when he offered me the job. I'm sorry. I'll have Joshua come and help you finish."

"You've been doing a fine job for us."

"Good to know."

"Luke, I'm sorry."

He glanced at her then. "Why should you be sorry? I'm the one who made a mistake. Many mistakes."

"It was Roy who made a mistake by repeating what you had told him. In his defense, he admires you greatly and wants to learn everything he can about you. I'm afraid he has a bad case of hero worship."

"And we both know I'm no hero, don't we?"

She didn't agree, but she was quiet for a long moment. Finally, she said, "You don't have to send Joshua to work in your place. I wouldn't be true to our faith if I turned you away because you weren't forthcoming about your parole. We forgive. We treat every man as a child of God. No man is sinless. We must not judge others lest we be judged ourselves."

A lump pushed up in his throat. "I don't deserve your kindness."

"Every man deserves kindness. I'm sorry you were embarrassed."

"I'm sorry I wasn't more honest."

"This parole thing you must do, is it the reason you have remained here?"

"*Ja.* Living at home and working in the family business is a condition of my parole. I could petition to move or get another job, but my parole officer would have to okay it."

"I see."

He picked up another board. "My sentence will be finished in a few weeks. After that, I'll be free to go anywhere, work anywhere, although jobs are scarce for ex-cons."

She folded her arms tightly across her middle. "So you will be leaving, then."

Hearing what he hoped was disappointment in her tone, he put down the board and walked up to her, stopping less than a foot away. "What would you have me do?"

She stared at her feet. "It isn't up to me."

"I know, but I'm asking. What would you like me to do? Stay, or go?"

She bit her lower lip. He wanted to kiss it. "You would make your family happy if you stayed among us."

He was putting her on the spot and that wasn't right. He stepped back and crossed to the stack of lumber to select a straight board. "*Ja*, it would make them happy if I stayed."

"That is important, but it is more important to seek God's will, Luke, not your own."

"Right. I'll tell Lillian about my situation and let her decide if she still wants me to help at the school."

"She will."

"How can you be so sure?"

"Because she is a woman of our faith. She lives it, as I try to do."

"Some of the parents may not feel the same. I wouldn't want to cause a problem for her."

It surprised and pleased Emma that he would put Lillian's concerns before his own. "If you feel you must tell her, I understand, but what you have told us doesn't need to leave this farm. I have told Roy that he is never to speak of it again."

Luke gazed at her with a soft light in his eyes. "I appreciate that, Emma. I do, but I'll tell Lillian tonight. What about you? I don't want to risk your reputation by working here."

"My father and my brothers are adequate chaperones. Don't worry about me."

He *was* worried about her—she could see it on his face—and some of the ice in her heart melted away. He must care about her a little.

Uncomfortable with the closeness that seemed to be pulling them together, she moved to where a shaft of sunlight from the open hayloft door highlighted a tarp covering something leaning against the barn wall. "What is this?"

"The solar panels I mentioned."

She lifted the tarp edge. The blue reflective surface and shiny aluminum frame glinted in the sunlight. "Will we be able to sell these if we can't use them?"

"Sure, but I'm really hoping we can use them. The English expect good lighting when they are shopping. Your father has a key cutter that could be run by solar electricity instead of your generator. You will need a cash register, too, and that takes electricity. If you have several battery-charging stations, folks could bring their car and marine batteries here, and you could expect a small fee for them to use it. Roy could recharge his cell phone at home instead of paying someone else."

Emma touched the gleaming surface and received an unpleasant jolt. The thing was dangerous. She dropped the tarp back in place and glanced at Luke sharply. "I told my brother to give his phone away."

"There's nothing wrong with him owning one."

"I hate how much he enjoys using worldly things. He wants a car. Father will never permit it."

"I had one when I wasn't much older than he is. I kept it at Jim Morgan's place so my folks wouldn't find out."

"I remember."

"You never would come for a ride with me."

"You forget, I watched you learning to drive. I saw you plow through the fence and drive across Jim's garden. It seems safer not to get in the car with you."

He laughed out loud. "That was my first day. I got better."

"You were so determined to learn."

"It was a skill I knew I would need when I left."

There it was again, the reminder that he never intended to stay in Bowmans Crossing. "Did you get your license?"

"Yup, for all the good it did me."

"What happened to your car?"

"I had Jim sell it and give the money to my parents when I was locked up. I knew they could use it."

"Someone recently saw you driving."

"I've done so once in a while. Jim Morgan has let me drive his Jeep for old times' sake. I hate to lose a skill I've learned, but it isn't something I plan to keep doing."

"Life rarely works out as we plan." She was walking proof of that. "That is why we must accept the will of God and let Him lead us."

"Why haven't you married, Emma?"

His personal question sent a rush a heat to her face. She stifled the urge to tell him it was none of his business. For some reason, she wanted him to understand. "The time never seemed right. My mother became ill and died suddenly not long after you were gone. Alvin and Roy were young and still needed me. My father was lost without *Mamm*. He needed me, too. I didn't have time for courting. After a while, the young men around here stopped asking."

"I've wondered about it. I couldn't see you spending your life alone. Not you. You are so full of life and light. My mother wrote to me every week, and I watched for news of you."

His tender words brought the sting of tears to her eyes. At least he had spared a thought or two for her after he left. She pulled the tattered remains of her hopes and dreams around her heart to shield it from the pain of wanting him to care. She couldn't let him see the power he still held over her.

"If you thought I was pining away for you, you were sadly mistaken. The best thing you ever did for me was leave without me."

He stepped closer to gaze into her eyes. "You don't know how many nights I prayed that was true. I'm glad to know I was right."

He was telling the truth. He believed he had done the right thing. Stunned by his revelation, Emma looked away.

"I have work to do." She left the hayloft and returned to the house. She took one look at the pile of dishes in the sink and ran upstairs to her room, slammed the door, fell on to her bed and cried her eyes out with her face buried in her pillow so no one could hear.

Chapter Nine

An hour later, Emma washed the last trace of tears from her face and went downstairs. She made short work of the dishes, put a chicken in to roast for supper and changed into her good dress. She wanted to be at the school when Luke spoke with Lillian. She would be there to support him no matter how painful it was. If he was to remain in their community, he had to see he would be accepted in spite of his flawed past.

And she did want him to remain. Up until now, she wouldn't have been able to admit that. Even to herself. Luke believed he had done the right thing leaving her behind. She still didn't know why, but it hadn't been because he didn't care. All these years she thought she had failed somehow. That she wasn't good enough, pretty enough or smart enough to be loved by him. Her greatest fear had been that he never really cared about her. That leaving her had been easy.

She walked through the door into the store. Two tall shelves, painted a bright white, were lined up down the center of the room. Luke was putting away his tools. She watched him for several minutes.

He wasn't the same man who had left so long ago. He was older. His face had the start of crow's feet and brow lines that hadn't been there when she first fell in love with him. She wasn't the same, either. She was quite familiar with her appearance. The mirror didn't lie. Crow's feet touched her temples, too. Her skin wasn't as fresh. Her eyes showed her worry.

It was time to stop acting like the child she had been. It was time to stop hiding behind the hurt. "Are you ready to go to school?"

"I am." As he approached, his eyes narrowed. He studied her face. "Are you all right?"

She wasn't about to admit she had been crying over him. "I have a small headache. It's nothing. The fresh air will cure it in no time."

"Should we take your buggy so you don't have to walk so far?"

"A brisk walk is exactly what I need. We should hurry. We don't want to keep the children later than we have to."

He nodded and held open the door for her. She slipped past him and started down the lane. Falling into step beside her, he remained silent for the first half mile. "Are you better? I can go back and get the buggy."

"Stop fussing, Luke. There are worse things in life than a little headache."

"Do you always help with the school Christmas program?"

"Every year. Lillian sometimes has trouble getting volunteers. She doesn't like to add to the workload of the children's parents, so she won't press them for additional help. I think she would find more people would step up if she had the bishop or the school board ask for volunteers. As it is, people see that the same few folk do the work every year and they don't feel there is a real need for them to do more."

"That's just human nature, I guess."

She glanced at him. "Why did you volunteer to help?"

"Timothy asked me, and I had nothing better to do."

That wasn't the answer she was hoping for. She wanted to hear him say he was eager to help his community, or the children, or to spread Christmas cheer.

Or spend more time with me.

Had he known that she would be helping? Or was it simply a coincidence? Maybe it was something more. Maybe he was interested in impressing Lillian. Her friend was single and pretty.

A tiny stab of jealousy hit Emma. She quickly subdued it. Lillian was a wonderful caring person. If she had caught Luke's eye, Emma could understand that.

She tried to gauge his interest in her friend. "Lillian is a wonderful teacher."

"Hannah likes her a lot." Luke leaned a little closer. "So does my brother Timothy."

Emma couldn't suppress the bubble of happiness that rose at his words. "I wondered about that. Timothy volunteering when he doesn't have a child in school has created some talk about the two of them."

"Is that a good thing, or a bad thing?"

"Honestly, it's just human nature."

"You know her pretty well. Do you think she would be interested in walking out with Timothy?"

Emma shot him a coy glance. "Are you his go-between?"

"Not officially. In fact, he hasn't said anything to me. Because you're her friend, I'm just trying to get a jump on the issue in case she has some objections or she is interested in someone else."

"There isn't anyone else, but you might warn Timothy that he may be facing an uphill battle."

"What makes you say that?"

"I have heard Lillian say that her desire is to remain single and to keep teaching school."

"That doesn't sound promising for my brother. I'll let him know."

She gave him a pleading look. "After Christmas?"

He chuckled. "All right. After Christmas."

Emma's heart lightened at the sound of his laughter. To her surprise, she found it made her happy to see him smiling. Perhaps they could be friends again. They weren't teenagers in the throes of first love anymore. That part of their relationship had been horribly painful, but it had been over years ago. If she truly forgave him, she had to let it go.

The school came into sight and he paused at the edge of the fence. "I want to thank you for doing this, Emma."

"For doing what?"

"For being my moral support. Maybe that wasn't your intention for coming with me, but having you here makes it easier."

"Then I'm glad I came."

"How is your headache?"

She pressed a hand to her temple. "It's completely gone."

"I reckon a walk in the fresh air was exactly what you needed, then."

He bent over, scooped up some snow and packed it into a ball. She watched in amusement as he took aim at the hapless snowman in the school yard. After a pitcher's windup, he let fly and knocked the tattered straw hat from atop his target. "Take that. Now who's going to step aside?"

Puzzled, she looked at him for an explanation. "What do you mean by that?"

"It's a little personal business between me and Frosty. Never mind. Shall we go in?"

"Only if you put the poor thing's hat back on and apologize. Violence never solves anything."

Laughing, Luke replaced the snowman's hat and brushed the loose snow off the scarf around his neck. "I'm sorry, sir, it will never happen again. You may melt into a puddle of slush at your leisure."

Emma walked past him, shaking her head. "I'm not sure that was an actual apology."

"Under the circumstances, it's all he's going to get."

Luke's good humor dried up when he walked into the building. Timothy was already building one of the frames he had promised. He and the three oldest boys had covered it with a piece of white canvas and began cutting it to size. They would staple it in place after the painting was finished. Lillian and the eighth-grade girls were testing paint colors on small strips of paper.

Luke glanced at Emma. She smiled and nodded encouragement. He walked across the room to the teacher's desk. "Lillian, I wonder if I might speak with you privately for a moment?"

Her eyebrows rose slightly. "Privately?"

Timothy scowled in his direction. Luke realized how bad that had sounded. A single fellow asking the teacher to step out with him alone in front of her students. "I meant that Emma and I would like to speak with you privately."

Lillian relaxed and turned to the girls watching her with interest. "I think the medium brown will work best for the walls of the inn and the stable. Try mixing a little white with the green paint we have to achieve a nice grass color. I'll be back in a few minutes."

She motioned for Luke and Emma to follow her outside, stopping to grab her coat by the back door. On the small stoop at the back of the school, she crossed her arms and waited.

Luke cleared his throat. "I should have told you this before I volunteered to work on your program. I'm sure you heard that I was in prison on drug charges."

"*Ja*, I have heard this."

"Most people think because I'm at home with my folks that I served my time and I'm free. That's not true. I'm still on parole. I'm still serving my sentence, although I get to do it in this community. I have rules I must follow or I can be taken back to prison. I understand if you feel I don't belong here with the *kinder*."

"Are you a danger to them?"

"I'm not. I promise you that. I like kids."

"I don't see that you are any different today than you were when you first offered to help us."

"Are you sure?"

"Completely."

"Danki." Relief sent his breath out in a whoosh.

Lillian glanced between Luke and Emma. "Can we get back to work now, or is there something else?"

Emma smiled brightly. "Nope, that's all."

"Goot. We have a lot to get done and not many days left to do it. Emma, would you see if there is more paint in the back of my buggy? I'm not sure the children brought it all in."

"Of course."

The second she was out of sight, Lillian rounded on Luke. "If you hurt her again, you will regret coming back here."

He knew what she was talking about and didn't deny it. "It's not my intention to hurt Emma. Ever."

"See that you don't."

Emma reappeared a few seconds later. "There's no paint in the buggy."

Lillian's smile was only for her friend. "Then we have it all. *Danki.*"

Luke followed the women inside and joined his brother. He smiled and winked at Timothy to let him know everything was okay. Timothy shrugged and went back to work.

After transferring Lillian's scene designs to the backdrops with a felt marker, Luke showed the girls how to use slightly darker or lighter shades of the same color to produce shadows and depth to their artwork. Emma had a steady hand and was able to draw the outlines of the many sheep dotting the hills.

When the girls were all busy, he left them and joined Timothy and the boys working on the second frame. Before long, he and the boys were all laughing over stories he and Timothy shared about building projects from their school days. Some of which had gone very wrong.

Lillian called a halt to the work and sent the children home before it grew dark. Timothy and Luke waited until Lillian and Emma were ready to leave, then they followed the women outside. At the road, the women walked up the road together. Luke waited and was rewarded with the sight of Emma looking back at him. He raised a hand, but she didn't wave. Still, he knew their relationship had taken a new turn.

"What are you grinning about?" Timothy asked and started walking toward home.

"Nothing." Luke pushed his hands in the pockets of his coat. The sun was just touching the horizon. Bands of low clouds were glowing with gold and pink colors that reflected off the snow in the fields, giving them pink hues as well.

"So what was your short personal conversation with Lillian about? I hope you didn't mention my name."

"Roy spilled the beans about my parole to Emma and her father. They were shocked, but Emma said it didn't matter. I was afraid it might matter to Lillian so I offered to step aside and let someone else help with the Christmas program."

"What did she say?"

"That I was the same person who offered to help. My situation didn't matter."

"I thought that's what she would say."

Luke glanced at him. "You like her a lot, don't you?"

Timothy's expression softened. "I do."

Luke didn't want to destroy his brother's hopes, but he felt he had to warn him not to get them too high. "Lillian likes being a teacher. If she were to wed, she would have to give that up."

"I'm not in a hurry to change things for her. We're friends. I just like being around her. Time will tell if we are meant to be together."

"I know what you mean," Luke said, thinking of Emma. He liked being near her, too. It was enough for now. He wouldn't push for more. Not yet.

"You mentioned Zachariah has some solar panels he might use or sell. I spoke with a friend from over near Berlin. His father makes furniture, but he also has a booming solar business sideline. I thought Zachariah might want to talk to him about it. Solar is gaining popularity, and a lot of Amish businesses are going to it because the lighting is safer than gas or kerosene and it's sure cheaper than running a diesel generator all day."

Luke looked at his younger brother with a newfound respect. "*Danki.* I'll tell him that. I didn't know you were interested in new technology."

"I'm not looking to run a television or a game console, but whatever we can do to make our business more profitable interests me. We employ six young men from the area now. Each one we hire means one less family has to move away to find work."

"You sound like Samuel."

"That's a nice compliment."

"How have you learned so much?"

"I like to read. If Zachariah decides he wants to use solar in his hardware store, he's going to have to get permission from the bishop first. I don't imagine everyone will be in favor of it. He should talk to the bishop on Sunday after the church service."

Luke sent Timothy a sidelong glance. "Doesn't it annoy you that we have to ask permission before making a change to our businesses?"

"*Nee*. Well, maybe just a little. But our ministers know that they must consider more than what benefits one family. Will this technology maintain our separation from the world? What impact will it have on our entire community? I tend to see the small picture. I'm glad there are prudent men who look at the big picture."

When had his younger brother developed into such a smart fellow? Luke admitted he was guilty of looking at the smallest picture. The one with only himself in the center. Maybe helping Emma and Zachariah with their business and the school with the Christmas program was letting him expand his view.

If Emma saw he wasn't the selfish fellow he'd once been, would it improve his chances with her, or would she still see Wayne as the better man?

She hated to admit it, but Emma missed having Luke around on Friday. Her father couldn't seem to settle on any task and very little got done in the store. It was only thanks to her nagging that she managed to get Roy to finish sanding one wall. The cans of primer and paint were never opened.

She was frosting a cake for supper when Alvin came in with the mail. "That looks yummy, Emma. I don't reckon I could have a slice now, could I? I'm mighty hungry."

She handed him the spatula loaded with frosting. "See if this will take the edge off your appetite. Does Lillian need me to come to the school this evening?"

He laid the mail aside and took the spatula from her, cleaning it with two licks. "*Nee*, tonight is the school board meeting so she wanted me to tell you to stay home."

"I expected as much. Go find your father and your brother, and tell them supper will be ready in five minutes."

"Is Luke here? Can he stay for supper?"

She shook her head. "He didn't come today."

"Is he coming tomorrow? I haven't had a chance to work with him here yet. He's loads of fun. He can sure tell some funny stories. Did you know that he and his brother Timothy nailed their teacher shut in the outhouse?"

Emma chuckled. "I remember that day very well. Luke was always getting into trouble." Sadly, while Luke was the instigator of some funny pranks, he often got his hapless followers in trouble, too.

After supper was finished and the dishes were done, Emma sat down in her chair in the living room to read the circle letter she had received from her mother's cousins in Pennsylvania. It was always fun to see what their faraway family was up to. She took out her old letter to them and set it aside. She would add her news and send the letters on to the next cousin until they got all the way around the family and back to the start. She read a particularly cute story about her cousin Millie's new baby and looked up to share it with her father. He was sitting in his recliner with a grim look on his face as he read his mail. "*Daed*, what's wrong?"

"It's a letter from my brother William. His wife passed away."

"*Aenti* Laura? How awful. Was she sick? They never mentioned as much."

"She had a stroke and died the next day. Her funeral will be on Tuesday."

"Are you going?"

"I don't see how I can. We don't have the money for that."

"You have been wanting to see your siblings. The boys and I can manage here."

"We can," Roy assured him.

She watched her father struggle with his decision. "I do want to see my brothers and my sister before…"

He didn't say *before it was too late*, but she knew that was what he meant. "Then go. Take our prayers with you and spend some time in Missouri."

She rose from her chair. "I'm going to go to the phone shack and make arrangements for a driver for you."

He laid the letter aside. "We can't afford to pay a driver for that long of a trip."

"We have enough money in the bank to cover this."

"As much as I want to go, I don't think I should. That money is for your dowry."

"Arthur Yoder came by the other day and asked if he could buy the old corn binder. You weren't here so I told him to come back later. He offered a good price. That will cover the cost of the trip, and I'll put the money back in the bank as soon as he pays me."

"*Nee*, the money from the farm equipment will go for your dowry. We decided this."

"I insist, Papa. You know you need to do this. I'll go make the call. You start packing."

"How will we get the store finished if I leave?"

She sighed in exasperation. "It can wait." Why was he being so stubborn?

"It can't. I have sent notices to the papers telling folks we'll be open for business the Monday after Christmas."

"Papa, why would you do that? We aren't ready." He could be the most irritating man.

"Because I wanted us to be ready."

Roy laid aside his magazine and came to stand at his father's side. "Luke and I can get it done. Don't worry."

In order to do that, Luke would have to come

over more than a couple of days a week. Would he do it if she asked?

"Roy is right," Emma agreed. Luke and Roy would get more done without her father underfoot. She would help, too. She knew how to wield a paintbrush and she could learn to price merchandise on shelves.

"Very well. You are right, Emma. I do need to go. This could well be my last chance to see them."

Alvin, sitting across the room, cocked his head to the side. "Why would it be your last chance, *Daed*?"

Her father cast a stricken glance in her direction. She forced a stiff smile to her lips and looked at her baby brother. "You father's brothers and sister are all older than he is. Who knows how long they will be with us."

"*Ja*, that is right." Her father nodded vigorously. "Roy, Alvin, your sister will be in charge. You must do as she says."

"But I'm the man of the house when you're gone. I should be in charge. I'm not in school anymore." Roy's eyes held a mutinous gleam.

"I'm older than you, so don't argue with your father about this." She brushed aside his hurt pride. She would deal with it later. For now, she had to get her dying father to his family in Jamesport, Missouri, as quickly and easily as possible and without alerting her brothers to what was wrong with their father.

Chapter Ten

Saturday morning dawned bitterly cold. Fresh snow was falling as Luke drove his buggy into Zachariah's yard. A white car sat in the driveway with the motor running. As he got down from his buggy, Luke saw the door to the house open. Zachariah and an English fellow Luke didn't know came out carrying a set of luggage. The driver put them in the trunk and opened the car door.

Zachariah spoke to him briefly and then approached Luke. "I was hoping to see you before I left."

"Where are you off to?"

"My sister-in-law has passed away. I'm going to her funeral in Missouri."

"I'm so sorry to hear this. You have my condolences." Luke looked over Zachariah's shoulder. "Are your children going with you?"

Zachariah shook his head. "I am going alone.

Emma and Roy are needed here to get the store open on time. I know I asked you to come here three days a week, but would you be able to come more? I don't think my children can do it all by themselves."

"That won't be a problem. I'll be here as often and for as long as they need me. Don't worry. I'll watch over them." It wasn't officially a new job, so it shouldn't matter to his parole officer, but he would send the man a note about it, anyway.

"*Danki.* I will let Wayne know that Emma is here with just the boys. I know he will want to stop in and check on her…on them as well."

"Of course."

"I must go. I appreciate your help, Luke. May God bless and keep you."

"And you as well. Safe travels." Luke watched Zachariah get in the car. A moment later, it drove away.

Luke walked up to the house and entered the kitchen. The Swartzentruber children were all sitting at the kitchen table with long faces. He pulled off his hat. "I'm sorry to hear of your loss."

Emma sat up straight. "It was God's will. Our aunt is with Him in Heaven now. There is no more pain and suffering for her. Roy, I want you to gather the eggs and feed the chickens and the horses. Alvin, I need you to milk the cow and feed the hogs."

Roy folded his arms across his chest and glared at her. "The chickens are your chores, Emma."

"I have other things I must do. Luke and I need to discuss what is needed to get the business open."

"I should be in on this discussion. It's going to be my business someday."

"Don't argue with me. Just go."

Roy shoved away from the table and stormed outside. Alvin got up, too. "Hi, Luke. I'm glad you're helping out. We're going to need somebody in charge."

"I am in charge, Alvin," Emma said. "You heard your father say that. Now get your chores done so you can help Luke finish painting the store."

Alvin had his back to his sister so she didn't see him roll his eyes. Luke smothered a smile as the boy walked past.

Luke twirled his hat in his hands. "Mutiny in your crew already?"

"Roy thinks he should be the one who was left in charge. I have been telling him what to do since he was a toddler. I don't see what difference it makes if *Daed* is here or not."

"Roy is almost an adult. You shouldn't treat him like a little child."

"As long as he is acting that way, that's how I will treat him. I need your support, Luke, not your criticism."

"I didn't mean to criticize, and you do have my support, Emma." He would do whatever he could for her and her family.

"Have a seat, Luke. Would you like some *kaffi*?"

"Your good coffee? Sure." He hung his hat on a peg by the door and returned to take a seat at the table. Emma filled a cup for him and then sat down across from him.

He took a sip. "Sure *goot*. As always."

"How did your parole meeting go, or would you rather not talk about it?"

"I don't mind." To his surprise, he didn't. "I met with Officer Merlin. We went over the paperwork that needs to be done for my release on December 24. He talked a lot about the reasons people like me end up in jail again. He wants to make sure that doesn't happen."

"People like you? Amish?"

"Drug users." He watched closely for her reaction. She flinched and he knew it was hard for her to accept, but he had to be brutally honest with himself.

"What reasons did Officer Merlin give?"

"A lack of support from families. Loneliness, feelings of isolation, inabilities to get and keep a job."

"You don't have those problems. Your family has supported you. You have a job."

"I have it better than a lot of people." He didn't

tell her how isolated and alone he felt at times. He didn't know anyone but Jim Morgan who had given up drugs and been able to stay clean. It was frightening how many of the people he knew had tried and failed.

He decided to change the subject. "Your father asked me to help get the store ready until he returns. I would've thought a funeral would be reason enough to stop work on it for a few days."

She swept a stray strand of hair back from her temple. "Father put notices in all the local papers announcing that we would be open on December 27."

"That's less than three weeks away. It won't be ready."

"The interior of the building is almost finished. What else do we need to do?"

"There's a lot of interior work to be done yet. The floor has to be laid. The walls and ceilings need sanding and priming before we can paint. More shelves have to be built. You'll need to stock the shelves, arrange and price your items. And decide on what kind of items you want to sell. You can't just offer boxes of random stuff that your father has stashed in his sheds and barns."

"What kind of things do you think we should offer?"

"All the things that people go to a hardware store to buy. Batteries, muckrakes, clotheslines, gas lamps, cooking utensils. You will need to find suppliers to sell to you on a regular basis."

"I'll have to start a list. This is overwhelming."

He reached across the table and covered her hand with his own. "It won't be easy, but if anyone can do it, I believe you can."

Her lips trembled as she smiled. "I will hold those words in my heart."

He couldn't ask for anything more. He squeezed her fingers. "You don't have to have everything done before you open your doors. If you offer the basics at a good price, people will be back and your father can gradually expand."

She pulled her hand away and looked down. Why did she suddenly look sad? "Emma, what's wrong? Don't tell me nothing. I can see something is troubling you."

"I am troubled, but there is nothing you can do to help me. I wish I could tell you about it, but I can't, so please don't ask again."

"All right. But if you find you want to talk, I can listen."

"Let's go take stock of what needs to be done. The time will go faster if I stay busy, and my father will be home before I know it."

He got up from the table and together they went to tour the building. Emma produced a notepad and jotted down the things they needed. After they were done, he could see that she felt even more overwhelmed. He didn't have a head for business, but she seemed to value his input. He hoped that he wasn't steering her wrong.

With the help of the boys, they soon had another set of shelves put together. By the end of the day, four new freshly painted shelves lined all the walls.

Emma looked around. "I think we should put a counter beside the front door where customers can pay for their purchases."

Luke nodded. They had accomplished a lot, but Emma still had a sad, worried look in her eyes when she thought he wasn't looking. When the boys were with them, she wore a stern, nononsense expression. Her curt comments annoyed Roy, but she didn't seem to notice, and Luke held his tongue.

After the evening meal was finished, Luke followed his father into the living room where a partially finished game of checkers sat waiting for them. Luke took his usual chair, and made the first move.

"Do you have any words of wisdom for me on how to help make Zachariah's business a success?"

His father frowned deeply. "*Nee*, I have no words of wisdom."

Luke realized his mistake at once. No Amish man would claim to have wisdom. Wisdom belonged to God and God alone. "I meant do you have some suggestions for me? You started our woodworking business from scratch. I value your advice."

Mollified, his father made his move. "When you go out to plant corn, do you plant it in winter?"

At one time, Luke would have been impatient with his father's roundabout way of answering a question, but he had learned to appreciate his father's methods. "I would plant corn in the spring when the earth begins to warm."

"Would you scatter the seeds on the ground?"

"Corn seed has to be planted one and a half to two inches into the soil."

"*Goot.* What comes next?"

"It must be cultivated to keep the weeds out."

"And when would you harvest it?"

"In the fall when the corn kernels are dry so they don't rot in the cribs."

His father nodded and jumped one of Luke's men. "That would be the best plan for corn."

"What would be the best plan for a hardware store?" Only after he made another move did Luke see his mistake.

"Now you are asking the right question." His father jumped two more men. "Crown me."

Luke complied. "Without a plan, I'm afraid Zachariah and Emma aren't going to know what to do next."

"If a farmer can teach you to grow corn…"

Luke sat up straighter. "Then a hardware-store owner can teach me about the hardware trade."

His father smiled. "A man has only one reason to invest his time and talent into a business. To provide for his family. I knew with five sons there wouldn't be enough farmland to support all of you. My goal was to grow a business where my sons and grandsons could work beside me and support their families. It was never about making money so that I could buy fancy things. It is, and always was, about keeping those I love near me."

Luke nodded. "That is Zachariah's aim as well, I think."

"Then it is likely that his efforts will prosper, too. Your mother has a cousin who owns a hardware store over by Mount Hope. He's a good fellow. I'm sure he'll be happy to show you and Zachariah the ropes." He took Luke's last checker from the board. "I win. Noah, are you up for a game?"

"Sure. I haven't had a sound beating in a week or more." He sank into a chair and redistributed the checkers.

Samuel, who had been working on the books in the corner of the room, got up and handed Luke a stack of magazines and books. Luke raised one eyebrow. "What's all this?"

"Information about operating a business, about

marketing, about taxes and hiring laws. A smart businessman never stops learning."

"I appreciate it, although I'm not sure when I'm going to have a chance to read all this."

"Anytime after you get our planer running again. It's stalled."

"The problem is that you don't love it enough, Samuel. Machines know who likes them and who doesn't."

A grunt was Samuel's only answer as he left the room.

Tomorrow was Sunday, and Luke wouldn't be able to work on the broken machine until Monday. Or he could do it tonight. Luke noticed his mother and Rebecca standing silently by the stove. His mother had a knowing smile on her face.

"What?" he asked, wondering why she looked so pleased.

"I was just giving thanks for answered prayers. Seeing my sons helping others and one another does my old heart good."

"I'm not sure how much help I'm giving Emma with Zachariah gone. I feel like I know less than she does. I'm afraid I may steer her wrong." And drain away Emma's dowry instead of increasing it. Not that he cared about the money.

With a start, he realized he was thinking about marriage. To Emma.

He glanced over his shoulder. All his brothers

were occupied. He chewed on his lower lip for a second as he stared at Rebecca.

His mother elbowed her. "He's getting up his courage."

Rebecca folded her hands in front of her. "He's pretty slow about it."

"He takes after his father."

Luke scowled at them. "This is serious."

Rebecca smiled. "I will happily be your go-between with my cousin Emma."

"What makes you think I was going to ask you that?" He didn't like the idea that the women in the house were one step ahead of him.

Rebecca and his mother exchanged glances and laughed. Between chuckles, his mother said, "We have been waiting for you to realize what it is that you want. All this talk of helping her make her business a success shows you've made up your mind."

He looked down at the book he held. "I guess maybe I have." Saying it meant he would stay in Bowmans Crossing, join the church, settle down and hopefully marry one day. Once he was a free man.

Rebecca gave him a sympathetic look. "We are all going to the cookie exchange. I'll find a time to speak to her alone then. You'll have your answer by Wednesday of next week."

Could it really be that easy?

Only if the answer was yes. If it was no, how did he deal with that?

Rebecca left the room and his mother came to his side. She pointed to the books he held. "In all your reading, I want you to remember one thing. Business is about relationships. Treat a customer right—he comes back. Treat him right again and he'll send his friend. It's not about what you can sell him today. It's about what he'll buy from you in his lifetime. Tell Emma she must not work in fear of failure. That is shortsighted. She should work as if she knows God will take care of it all. Because He will."

"I'll share that with her."

"It is a lesson you should learn, too, my son."

"What do you mean?"

"If you live in fear of failure, you doubt God's goodness and mercy. Fear steals your strength."

He did live in fear. Fear of failure, fear of returning to drugs. Could he find the faith, the strength, to believe God would not let that happen to him again? He had to or he couldn't ask Emma to consider him. He had to be sure, for her sake as well as his own.

Emma sat beside Roy as he turned in at the Aaron Miller farm. Dozens of buggies were already lined up on the hillside west of the barn. The horses, still wearing their harnesses, were tied up along the fence. Most stood dozing in the sun while others were content to munch on the hay spread in front of them until they were needed to return home.

The bulk of the morning's activity was focused around the barn. Aaron Miller's home was too small to accommodate all the church's family members. The service would be held in his barn.

The men of the community were busy unloading backless seats from the large gray boxlike bench wagon that was used to transport the benches from home to home for the services held every other Sunday. Bishop Beachy was supervising the unloading. When the wagon was empty, he joined his two ministers, and they all approached the house.

Emma entered the farmhouse ahead of them. Inside, it was a beehive of activity as the women and young girls arranged food on counters and tables. The smaller children were being watched over by elder sisters or cousins. She knew Alvin would be outside with the young boys, playing a game of tag. Roy would find his friends to gossip with and watch the girls bringing food inside.

Catching sight of her Aunt Ina visiting with Rebecca, Emma crossed the room toward them and handed over her basket of food. *"Guder mariye."*

"Good morning," Rebecca replied, taking the basket from her. "Isn't this weather nice? I hope it lasts."

Emma said, "I see the bishop and the ministers coming already. We should hurry." Bishop Beachy and his two ministers entered the house and went upstairs to one of the bedrooms. There they would discuss the preaching for the day. Nothing would be written down.

The service would last for approximately three hours and all the preaching would be done from memory alone. Amish ministers had no formal training. They spoke from the heart, as they believed God inspired them.

When Emma reached the barn with her aunt and cousin, she saw it was already filled with people sitting quietly on rows of backless wooden benches. The women sat on one side of the aisle and men on the other side. Tarps and blankets had been hung over ropes stretched between upright timbers to cordon off an area for the service. The sounds of cattle and horses could be heard from the nearby stalls.

Rebecca and Ina took their places among the married women. Emma spied Lillian among the unmarried women and went to join her. She looked about for her brothers and saw them sitting in the back row on the men's side as close to the open door as they could get. The moment the service was finished, they would rush out.

From the men's side of the aisle, the *Volsinger* or song leader announced the first hymn. There was a wave of rustling and activity as people opened their thick songbooks. The *Ausbund* contained the words of all the hymns the Amish used, but no musical scores. The songs were sung from memory, passed down through countless generations. They were sung slowly and in unison by people opening their hearts and minds to receive God's presence without the distraction of musical instruments. The elderly man started the hymn in a clear, sweet voice that reminded Emma of Alvin's voice. The rest of the congregation joined in, and she could hear Alvin singing loud and strong behind her. She couldn't pick out Roy's voice and knew he was mumbling his way through. He hated singing. She tried to pick out Luke's voice, but couldn't.

At the end of the first hymn, Emma took a moment to glance toward the men's side. She spotted Luke sitting just behind the married men. His unmarried brothers sat near the back while Joshua and Samuel sat beside their father. Luke glanced in her direction, and she smiled at him. He smiled back and then focused on his songbook. The song leader announced the second hymn: *"O Gott Vater, wir Loben dich* (O God the Father, We Praise You)." It was always the second hymn of an Amish service.

Emma forgot about Luke and her brothers as she joined the entire congregation in singing God's praise, asking that He allow the ministers to speak true to His teachings, and praying that the people present would receive His words and take them into their hearts.

At the end of the second hymn, the ministers and Bishop Beachy came in. They hung their black hats on pegs set in the wall for that purpose. It was the signal that the preaching was about to begin. Nearby, a young child began to fuss. His mother slipped a string of beads and buttons from her purse and gave them to her little one. He quieted and played with his toy, chewing on it and shaking it while his mother focused on the preachers.

Emma tried to listen closely to what was being said, but she found her mind wandering. She thought of her father and prayed for his healing. She asked God to grant her patience to deal with Roy and she prayed for Luke, that he would find peace and acceptance within the community. Finally, she prayed to accept God's will if it was His desire that she marry as her father wished. Wayne was a good man and he would make a good husband. It wasn't his fault that he didn't make her heart race. Marriage had to be about more than simple physical attraction. It was about hard work, respect. and duty to God and church.

When the service was finally over, Emma joined the women in the house as they prepared a luncheon. The men stacked the backless benches to make tables and the food was laid out for people to help themselves. The ministers and elders were served first. The youngsters played games outside until it was their turn to eat.

Luke came inside with Noah and Timothy when it was their turn. Emma was filling glasses with lemonade and cups with black coffee for those who wished it. Luke took a glass of lemonade from her. "I would like to speak to you when you're done here."

She looked around. "I think they can spare me for a few minutes."

He looked pleased. "Why don't we step outside?"

Her heart started hammering wildly. Was he about to ask her to ride home with him? Would she accept? "Let me get my cloak."

He walked out but before she could follow, Lillian caught her by the arm. "Emma, what are you doing?"

"Luke wants to have a word with me."

"If he asks to drive you home and you let him, you are a bigger fool than I would have believed possible."

"I know you think he treated me badly in the past."

"I don't *think* it. I saw it. You cried on my shoulder for hours that night."

"The other day you didn't have any objections to him working with the children."

"I don't object to him helping his community. I do have an objection to him breaking your heart again. He's not worth it, Emma. You can do better."

She glanced out the window where Luke was waiting on the porch. "What if I don't want to do better?"

What if Luke was the man she wanted? How could she know if he was the man God had chosen for her?

Chapter Eleven

Luke waited for Emma to come outside. He was already more nervous than he had been since the first time he asked the girl if he could drive her home after a Sunday-evening singing. That girl had been Emma and he had been a nervous sixteen-year-old. Why couldn't Rebecca find a way to speak to her today? Why did he have to wait? He wasn't good at waiting.

What answer would Emma give Rebecca? Would she be willing to go out with him or would he find out that Wayne was her choice. He tried to prepare himself to hear that answer.

He looked through the window and saw her talking to Lillian. Both women wore serious expressions. Lillian stood with her arms crossed and a scowl on her face. It deepened when she caught sight of him. There was more than a friendly conversation going on. His hopes took a nosedive. Lillian might think it was all right for him to make Christmas decorations for the school, but he knew dating Emma would be a different story. Was she telling Emma as much?

"Luke, it's good to see you this holy day. How have you been?"

He turned to see Bishop Beachy approaching. "I've been well and hoping to speak to you."

"I just heard from Roy that you are helping to finish Zachariah's store while he has traveled to his sister-in-law's funeral in Missouri. I will spread the word so that others may offer their condolences. Do his children need anything?"

"A few extra hands to help finish the store before he returns would be wonderful."

"I and my boys will come by this week. I'm sure I can find a few more volunteers, too."

"That would be a blessing. Speaking of volunteers, I believe Lillian Keim could use a few extra hands getting the school ready for the Christmas program."

"Really? She hasn't mentioned this to me."

"My brother Timothy and I built part of her set, but I overheard her say she could use more help making the costumes."

The door to the house opened. Emma came outside with Lillian right behind her. The bishop turned to address them. "My condolences on your loss, Emma. With your father gone, you can depend on our community for any help."

"Danki."

"You will find many willing hands at your door this week to finish Zachariah's store. Teacher Lillian, Luke tells me that you require more help with the costumes for the Christmas play. My wife and my daughters-in-law will be happy to assist, as will other women. You must not think you need to do all the work yourself. You must allow others the joy of making our Christmas program a success, too."

Luke caught the look of surprise Lillian cast in his direction. She blushed slightly and dropped her gaze to her clasped hands. "I know the women of our community are especially busy this time of year getting ready for Christmas, Bishop. Many are cleaning to make ready for out-of-town visitors, baking for their families and for others. I hate to take them away from their tasks."

"Those who cannot spare the time are excused, but those who do have a few extra moments on their hands will be glad to do something to benefit our *kinder*. I will spread the word. When should they meet with you?"

Lillian nodded once. "*Danki*, Bishop Beachy. Anyone who can help should come to the school on Tuesday at one o'clock."

"I'll pass on the message. Now I must see Aaron Miller and congratulate him. I hear he had a new grandson in Illinois."

Luke spoke quickly. "Before you go, sir, Emma and I have one more concern."

"What is it?"

Luke waited for Emma to speak; when she didn't he charged ahead. "Zachariah has a number of solar panels that he has collected."

The bishop laughed. "That doesn't surprise me."

Luke grinned, too. "They would provide electricity for the store if you were to approve their use."

Slipping his thumbs beneath his suspenders, the bishop slid them up and down. "I have heard from other bishops that there is a great deal of interest in this new technology. Some communities have already embraced it. I'm afraid I can't give you permission to use it without further study. This year's regional bishops' meeting is being held next week. I will seek the counsel of others on this matter and render a decision after that."

"It uses God's sunlight. It doesn't connect us to the outside world," Luke said, hoping to sway him to their side.

Smiling gently, the bishop nodded. "As you know, we Amish sometimes embrace a new invention only to find it does not promote our way of life. When I was a small boy, our community allowed the new telephones into our homes. It appeared on the surface to be a *goot* thing. A way to keep in touch with our families and to summon help in an emergency. For a while, it worked, but many soon began to notice people were spending too much time talking with others, not about business, but in gossip and other ways that were not beneficial to our people. The bishops met and agreed having a phone for emergencies was essential, but not in every home. My mother cried when my father took our phone out. We only have a community phone booth now. As others use solar power, they will gain a better understanding of its benefits and problems, and they will share what they have learned at the bishops' meeting."

"Thank you for considering it," Emma said.

The bishop turned to Lillian. "Come with me and speak with my wife about what is needed for the school."

When they were out of earshot, Emma smiled at him. "That was very kind of you to think of getting more help for Lillian."

"I didn't want you to worry about her since you aren't able to help as much now that your father is gone."

"I appreciate that, Luke. What did you want to speak to me about?"

He glanced around and noticed they were getting a few stares and frowns from some of the older members and his courage failed him. "I wanted to ask if you'd like to check out the hardware store over by Mount Hope. The owner is my mother's second cousin. My father says he'll be happy to show us how to run a hardware business."

"Sure. When?"

She smiled shyly at him and his hopes soared high once more. A long buggy ride without prying eyes on them was a better place to speak of courting than this. "The sooner the better. I'll be at your place bright and early tomorrow."

"I'll see you then."

She had to like him. But did she like him enough to agree he could come courting?

"Emma, get your coat."

She looked up in surprise when Luke came rushing into the house on Monday morning. "My coat? Why?"

"Because we are going shopping."

"For what?"

"Experience and information. Hurry, it's a long drive and it looks like it could snow." He rushed out the door.

She got her coat and followed him, but she didn't get in the buggy. "I still don't understand what we are doing. We need to be here to direct the men working inside."

"There were already five men working with Roy in the store. Roy knows what needs to be done. Get in."

Exasperated, she climbed in the buggy and

shut the door. A basket with warm bricks at her feet kept the chill away. "At least tell me where we're going."

Luke slapped the reins against the horse's rump. "I already told you. The hardware store in Mount Hope."

"I didn't think you meant we'd go rushing off first thing this morning."

"My father said if I wanted to grow corn, I should talk to a farmer, and if I wanted to run a business, I should talk to someone in the business."

He seemed so pleased with himself that she couldn't help but smile. "Let's hope your mother's cousin is a good businessman."

"Amen to that."

They rode in silence for a while with the steady clip-clop of the horse's hooves and the hum of the tires on the road the only sounds to fill the void. She had so many questions that she wanted to ask him, yet she didn't know how to start. Why had he left her behind? Why wasn't her love good enough for him? Had there been someone else? An English girl?

As often as she told herself the past no longer mattered, the same questions came back to nag her.

"How is Roy doing with your father gone?" Luke glanced at her.

Her family was a safer subject than her past

hurts. "He hasn't been an easy person to have around. He resents every task I give him."

"What does he want to do?"

"I don't know."

"Maybe you should ask him."

She scowled at him. "He wants to be in charge."

"Maybe you should let him."

"He's only a boy. I'm overwhelmed with all that needs to be done. How can he possibly hope to know what is needed?"

"Roy has spent a lot of time with your father. He knows what Zachariah has in the sheds. If you ask him he can tell you what is broken and what just needs a little work."

"If you have so much faith in him, why didn't you bring him instead of me?"

"He wanted to get started on the floors."

"I will admit he had done a lot of work already. I know the business will be his one day, but will he be an Amish or an *Englisch* businessman when that day comes?"

"Only your brother can make that decision. You can't make it for him."

Emma bit back a retort, knowing he was right. She stared at the window at the passing scenery. Snow covered the shocks of corn stacked in the fields. It clung to the backs of horses and cattle grazing by the fences. "I know it seems like I nag, but I can't help it. I want so much for him to be happy with our simple ways."

"I can understand that."

She glanced at him. "Are you happy with your Amish life now or do you long to return to the world?"

"I'm finding…contentment." He looked at her and smiled, but something in the way he said it made her doubt him.

"Is that enough?"

"I pray it will be."

She fell silent, not knowing what else to say. It wasn't too much later that they pulled into the parking lot of the Big River hardware store.

There were three hitching posts out front for buggies as well as parking spaces for cars. Two buggies and three cars occupied spaces. "I wish I'd brought my notebook."

"One like this?" Luke pulled a notepad from his pocket and handed it to her along with a pencil. She smiled her thanks. "You've thought of everything."

Flipping it open, she wrote *hitching rails* and *parking spaces*.

Luke got out and came around to open the door for her. She grasped his hand to get down, and even with gloves on she could feel the energy that seemed to arc between them. Almost like the jolt she had received from the solar panel. After that, she made a point to avoid touching him. It was already hard to concentrate when he was near.

Inside the building, she met his mother's cousin and they were soon being treated like honored guests. Albert Chupp and his wife, Esta, answered Emma and Luke's questions, showed them how they kept track of inventory and wrote down the names of the suppliers they used. Emma had already thought of stocking lamps and lampshades, but she hadn't considered the need for yards of cotton wick material or the replacement wheels that fed the wicks into the lamp. Nor did she have any idea that there were so many sizes of screws and bolts to be had.

By the time they left, she had pages and pages of her notebook full of simple items they could carry and tips for displaying merchandise. As she climbed back into the buggy, she sighed heavily. "There's no way we can have a place like this."

Luke got in and picked up the reins. "Don't work in fear. Work as if God has everything under control because He does."

She studied the building in front of her. "I reckon I'll have to try. How am I going to make the outside of our store as inviting as theirs?" Patio furniture was grouped to one side while birdbaths and stacks of garden pottery lined the other side of the building. Her father's store was much smaller. They wouldn't have room for such big items.

"A little more color will help. Some of your colored lamps in the window along with pretty shades."

"You're right. Something bright. It will come to me."

"Of course it will. You're one of the smartest women I know."

Her mouth dropped open at his compliment, but she quickly snapped it shut. He thought she was smart. Was she, or was she being foolish to hope he cared for her? He was being helpful—there was no denying that—but why? Was it because he cared about her?

Luke hoped he had done the right thing by bringing Emma with him. He didn't want to discourage her, but she had to know what was involved in running a business like the one Zachariah was intent on starting. He regretted his decision to let Roy remain at home, but Luke was still working up the courage to ask Emma out. He didn't want her brother in on that conversation. Next time, he would take the boy with him and let him see what kind of business his father was getting into, too.

Emma was quiet on the way home. She sat reading and rereading her notes. He glanced at her often, happy to simply be traveling with her. It amazed him that she didn't have to do anything or say anything and he still enjoyed being near her.

Isn't that what love is?

He listened to the small voice in his heart, knowing he was truly falling in love with Emma. It wasn't the mad passion they had shared as teens. That passion was still there—he felt it whenever he looked at her or thought of her—but this new gentleness carried with it much richer emotions. Even so, he couldn't act on those feelings until he was certain he belonged among the Amish. He had to know staying was God's will for him. And he needed to know Emma's feelings about Wayne.

He sighed deeply as he realized he couldn't ask her out until he had those answers.

"Can we see some solar panels while we are out?" she asked.

"Sure. Timothy said he knows a man near Berlin that sells them. It's not too far out of our way."

"I think one of those we have is defective."

"Why do you say that?"

"Because it shocked me just as hard as Jim Morgan's electric fence."

"Was the sun shining on it at the time? They produce electric power even in dim light."

"Now you tell me. Are they dangerous? Can they start fires?"

"I don't know."

"These are things we must investigate before we install them for our new business."

"I agree."

"Goot."

"You're getting kind of bossy, aren't you?" There was a hint of challenge in his tone.

She gaped at him. "I am not."

"My mistake. I've been listening to Roy too much."

"Roy says that I'm bossy?"

"He says you are always coming down hard on him."

"The boy knows how to make me angry. I can't seem to stop harping at him. I know I'm doing it, but he pushes until he gets that reaction from me."

Luke tried to draw on some of his feelings and mistakes as a kid. "Give him more responsibility. Let him fail if he doesn't get it right. He'll learn more that way than you telling him he's wrong."

"I wish my father were here."

"You're doing a fine job. Just lighten up on Roy."

Emma gritted her teeth to keep from replying to his suggestion. He didn't have to deal with an unruly teenager day in and day out. He had been the unruly teenager.

Her fair-mindedness asserted itself. Maybe he did have a special understanding that she lacked because of his own teenage years. She would follow his suggestion and see if it made a difference. She wasn't getting anywhere with Roy by doing it her way.

It didn't take long to reach their second destination of the day. The furniture maker with a solar sideline turned out to be a jovial Amish fellow by the name of Reuben Kaufman. Emma discovered he sold all the usual Amish-made furniture along with solar-powered garden lights, solar panel kits and fence chargers.

"A while back Amish people frowned at solar power. But now they see all the good it can do. I've run my cash register and key-cutting machine for ten years on solar alone. This summer I'm going to upgrade from my four small panels to eight larger panels. I've got this paint-mixing machine that takes a lot of energy. Gets expensive running my diesel generator all day."

Luke asked a question about fuses, voltage and amps that left Emma completely in the dark. After that, the conversation turned technical. She had very little idea what they were discussing. Luke, on the other hand, appeared to be thoroughly enjoying himself. She was astonished and a little bit uneasy at how well he understood the workings of the solar panels. He seemed more *Englisch* than Amish when he talked about the potential of solar energy. He was eager to learn everything he could. When Reuben mentioned there was a school to teach installation, Luke took particular note, jotting down the address and the phone number.

On their way home, she questioned his interest in the school. "Are you going to become a solar installer?"

"There's no sense in selling something people can't use. I was thinking it might be something that would interest Roy. He likes gadgets. With a certified installer, you could sell and install small panels for things like battery-powered fence chargers to keep cattle in. With a large enough array, a fellow could run a sewing machine, a vacuum, or a water pump and still have enough juice left over to charge the batteries for his buggy lamps. Imagine while you are working in the sun, the sun is working for you by charging your batteries so you would never have to buy gas or diesel to run a generator."

"This all seems much too fancy."

"Now you sound like Wayne. Very old-fashioned."

"There's nothing wrong with Wayne's opinions. They are shared by many others."

"By you?"

"In some cases." She closed her mouth, refusing to argue with him.

"Then you should make a good pair."

"I have told you nothing is decided between us."

"But you are still considering him."

"Because father wishes it."

"Right." He clicked his tongue and put the tired horse into a trot. Emma didn't object. She was every bit as eager to get home as he was. And why wouldn't he be? He thought she was bossy and old-fashioned and all but married to Wayne Hochstetler.

Luke Bowman didn't know her well at all. And she barely knew him anymore. Could that change or would they always be on edge with each other?

Chapter Twelve

With the help of the bishop, his sons and several other men from the church district, the inside of her father's shop was completed within a week. Late one morning, Emma left the last batch of chocolate-mint cookies she had baked for the cookie exchange cooling on the counter and walked through the store in amazement.

The ceiling was painted a bright white. Two skylights kept the interior from being dark. The walls were painted a soft mint green that made her think of summer and green apples. Two dozen shelves stood in rows waiting for merchandise. The wide-plank pine floors gleamed with wax. She would put a pen to paper tonight and describe for her father all that had been accomplished. The next step was filling the shelves. She pulled out her notebook and began to make notes about where things should go.

Shouting from outside drew her attention

sometime later. She walked to the bay window and looked out but didn't see anything. Pulling on her coat, she went outside and followed the noise to the west side of the house. Roy and Alvin were engaged in a running snowball battle around the henhouse. Luke stood a few feet in front of her, laughing at their antics. She had a perfect view of his broad back.

Opening her mouth to scold her brothers for playing when they should be working, she held her tongue instead. Luke's advice to stop being so hard on Roy kept her silent. Everyone had been working hard. Maybe it was time for a little fun.

She glanced down at the sparkling snow by her boots and scooped up a handful. It was perfect for making snowballs. The sun had melted it just enough so that it packed together nicely. Quietly, she added another handful, making the ball she held almost the size of a softball. Hefting it from hand to hand, she stared at Luke's back. It would be an easy shot.

"Don't even think about it." He hadn't turned around. How did he know?

"Don't think about what?" She feigned innocence and hid the ball behind her back.

He glanced over his shoulder. "You'll be sorry."

"Not as sorry as you'll be." She threw the snowball. It struck his shoulder, sending an explosion of icy crystals into his neck and face.

"That wasn't nice, Emma Mae."

A giggle escaped her. "Maybe not, but it was remarkably satisfying."

Slowly, he brushed the snow away. "You know what has to happen now."

"You must turn the other cheek." She scooped a handful at him and bolted toward the house.

She didn't make it five feet before he retaliated with a hit to the back of her head. She scrunched her neck against the cold sensation of snow sliding down beneath her collar. "Argh."

"Told you that you'd be sorry."

Glaring at him, she turned around. "This means war."

He held up both hands. "Turn the other cheek, Emma. You'll feel terrible if you don't."

Roy and Alvin had stopped and were watching. She hefted a new snowball and motioned slightly with her head. Roy nodded and grinned. He and Alvin left the henhouse and advanced quietly from the rear with a snowball in each hand.

To keep Luke's attention. She planted one hand on her hip and held her snowball aloft like a shot put. "I will consider turning the other cheek after I hear an apology."

"I'm sorry you hit me with a snowball first."

"Not good enough."

"I'm sorry you can't throw very well."

"I hit what I was aiming at."

"I think you wanted my face but got my shoulder." He took a step toward her.

Hopping back, she shook her head. "No, you don't. You aren't going to stuff snow down my back."

"The idea never crossed my mind. Until you mentioned it." He gave a deep laugh and advanced steadily.

She turned as if to flee, but spun back quickly enough to slap the snow in his face as he ran at her. He stopped and shook like a dog. "You are going down, and you are going to eat snow, girl."

Giggling, she hopped from side to side, daring him to catch her. In a singsong voice, she chanted, "I have something you don't have. I have something you don't have."

"And what would that be?"

"My brothers behind you."

He spun around and ducked as Roy and Alvin threw with both hands. The snow hit Emma in the face and chest. She stood in openmouthed shock at the cold.

Luke and her brothers were laughing so hard they couldn't stand up. Luke was rolling with mirth. Turning slowly around, Emma walked back to the store and lifted one of her father's grain shovels from the rack. She walked outside, scooped up a shovelful, rounded the corner and dumped it on Luke. Her brothers scrambled to their feet, but she already had a second scoop loaded and she flung it toward them, showering them with white powder.

"I give up." Luke was still laughing as he pulled his coat off to shake the snow out.

Her brothers took off firing at each other again.

Luke came toward her with his hands up. Something in his eyes alerted her to his intentions, but it was too late. He dove at her, carrying her into a nearby snowdrift. His fingers around her wrists prevented any retaliation. She was forced to lie in the cold snow until he released her.

The playful gleam in his eyes slowly vanished. His pupils darkened. "I think we should kiss and make up, don't you?"

Slowly, he leaned down.

Emma knew he was going to kiss her. If she turned her head to the side, it would be a simple peck on the cheek, part of the game, but she didn't turn her face. She licked her lips, tasting the cold snow, and closed her eyes.

She could feel his warm breath on her lips, but he didn't touch them. She lifted her face ever so slightly in invitation. He groaned and rolled away from her. Disappointment stabbed through her, followed by shame.

Sitting up, she pulled her coat tight at her throat. He lay on his back looking up at the sky. "I'm sorry."

"For what? Nothing happened. It was a silly game that got out of hand."

He raised his head to look at her. "I wanted it to get out of hand."

So had she, but she didn't admit it. Wasn't she pretty enough? Wasn't she tempting enough? Why was she forever wanting him and he was forever turning away? It was cruel.

He rose to his feet and held out his hand. "Truce?"

She knocked his hand aside, pleased by the look of shock on his face. Rising to her feet, she stomped toward the house to change. He caught her by the arm. "Emma, wait."

"Let me go." She tried to jerk away, but he held her fast.

"I'm not sure what I did wrong." He sounded so pathetic that she almost felt sorry for him. Almost.

"You didn't do anything wrong. Now, let go of me."

"I did something to upset you. I'm sorry. Emma, I respect you. I would never dally with your affections."

"You don't want to kiss me, that's fine. Don't make a big deal out of it."

He tipped his head slightly. "Wait, you're mad because I didn't kiss you?"

"Let it go."

"*Nee*, not till I've righted a wrong." He pulled

her into his arms and kissed her soundly. His lips moved over hers with a skill that left her breathless. He tasted of mint and chocolate. When her knees grew weak, he pulled away as breathless as she was.

"Was that better?"

She touched her tingling lips with her fingertips. "You've been snitching cookies."

He threw up his hands. "Busted. Haul me away. Your brothers gave me some."

She smoothed her dress and straightened her *kapp*. "Stay out of my kitchen. In fact, go home. We're done for the day."

"Okay." He took a step back, stumbled and sat in the snow.

She marched into the house, went up the stairs and straight to her room. After closing the door, she lay down on the bed and pressed her fingers to her lips again. That had been a very fine kiss.

Luke got up, dusted off his pride and began walking home. He was almost to the covered bridge when Joshua and Mary drove past in their buggy. Joshua drew the horse to a stop. "Need a ride?"

Luke shook his head. "I need to walk."

"What's wrong?"

"Women. When someone understands them, let me know. No offense, Mary."

"None taken. Joshua, I'll drive on to school

and get Hannah. Why don't you walk your brother home? He looks like he can use some company."

Joshua handed the reins to his wife and got out. She drove away and he turned to Luke. "Women troubles?"

"Woman. One woman. Emma."

"Let's hear your side of the story before Mary gets it out of Emma."

"It all started so innocently."

"It always does."

"One minute I was chucking snowballs at an old friend. The next minute, I was lying next to her in the snow acting like a scoundrel. I got up before anything happened, and she got mad."

"Most women don't like a man to act like a scoundrel."

"That's not it. She was mad because I didn't kiss her."

"Odd."

"You're telling me."

"What did you do?"

"I kissed her."

"Luke, I have to tell you that might have been the wrong move. Did she slap you?"

He shook his head. "She accused me of swiping cookies and told me to go home."

"That's it?"

Nodding, Luke pulled off his hat. "That's it. It

was like I was five again." He raked his fingers through his hair.

"You got off easy, *brudder*."

"Joshua, give me a reason for her actions that I can wrap my brain around."

"I'm no romance expert."

"Are all women as confusing as Emma is?"

"I have no idea. If I were you, I'd pretend it didn't happen."

"I can try that." But he knew that it wouldn't work. He was never going to forget the feel of her soft lips against his.

What do you want me to do, Lord? Is she the one, or am I kidding myself? I need Your help, Heavenly Father. Show me what You desire for me.

The two men walked in the back door of their father's house and were immediately surrounded by the aroma of gingersnaps, snickerdoodles, chocolate-chip cookies and oatmeal-raisin bars.

They looked at each other and smiled. "Cookie exchange."

Joshua peeked around the corner of the kitchen. "I'll distract *Mamm*, you grab as many cookies as you can and I'll meet you in the barn. Deal?"

Before they could make a move, their father bolted out of the kitchen with his hand covering his head. "I only took one."

"And that is the last one you will see until next

Christmas." Their mother stopped in the doorway with a rolling pin in her hand. "What are you boys doing here?"

Joshua being closest took a step back. "Nothing, *Mamm*. We're—nothing, *Mamm*."

"Go make yourselves useful. The buggy needs to be washed."

"On it," Luke assured her.

"Hmmph!" She raised one eyebrow, spun on her heels and went back to the kitchen.

Joshua tried to see the top of his father's head. "Did she get you?"

"Missed me by a hair. This hair." He pulled a silver strand straight up.

Luke looked toward the kitchen and then gathered the others into a huddle. "She can't get all of us. If we rush her, we can snag a bunch of those awesome gingersnaps and get out before she knows who to swing at."

"Sounds like a plan. Which side of the table shall I take?" Joshua asked.

"What are you guys up to?" Timothy came strolling in from the kitchen with a cookie in each hand.

"How did you get those?" his father demanded.

"These?" He held out his cookies. "I asked *Mamm* if I could have one. She gave me two."

Luke's father turned and looked at each of his sons in turn. "He asked."

"I still say we rush her." Joshua rubbed his hands together.

"Shall I go get some for you?" Timothy offered.

"She won't let you have them. They're for the cookie exchange."

"Sure she will." Timothy handed his uneaten cookie to his father and went back to the kitchen. He came out a few minutes later with a plate of assorted cookies. "You just have to ask nicely, guys."

Luke took one from the plate. "Stealing them is more fun." It was the same with kisses, too, but how much better would it be to have Emma give them freely? He had to know how she felt about him.

Emma waited impatiently in the kitchen for Wayne to arrive with his daughter on the evening of the cookie exchange. Maybe some time with Wayne's daughter would get the memory of Luke's kiss out of her mind. It was all she could think about. What had it meant to him? Had it meant anything? She touched her lips again. Had he felt the same thrill that raced through her nerve endings?

Would Wayne's kiss thrill her in the same way? Wayne was everything that Luke was not. Steady, dependable, grounded in the Amish life and faith. He would make any woman a good husband. If she wasn't so foolish, she would encourage Wayne's attention.

But the only man whose attention she wanted was Luke. Not dependable. Not a member of her faith. Not good husband material. Why couldn't she get over him?

Now that the store was finished, she wouldn't see him as much. That was for the best. She needed to concentrate on helping her father and her brothers in the coming months.

Roy came through the room with a rolled up magazine under his arm. "What's for supper?"

"I've got ham and beans on the stove. You and Alvin can just help yourselves when you're ready. What are you reading?"

He pulled the periodical out and held it up for her inspection. "It's a magazine that tells you how to set up solar arrays, how to install them and how to wire them. Luke gave it to me. It's really cool. He said I might be able to go to school to learn this."

"Luke shouldn't promise things he can't control. Your father and the bishop will have to decide if it is acceptable. What if we can't afford it?"

"Luke didn't promise anything. We just talked about it. Don't forget to bring back lots of cookies." He tucked the magazine under his arm and went outside.

Emma heard a buggy arrive a few minutes

before five. Wayne was prompt. Another point in his favor. Going to the door, she held it open. He stepped down from the buggy and lifted out his child. She held a small white plastic pail to fill with cookies.

Wayne walked to the door. "Emma Swartzentruber, this is my daughter, Sophie. Sophie, this is my friend Emma. She is taking you to the cookie exchange tonight."

Emma knelt to put herself at the child's level. "Hello, Sophie. I'm pleased to meet you. We're going to have so much fun. There will be lots of *kinder* there for you to play with and good things to eat."

Blond with pale blue eyes, Sophie held on to her father's leg and looked painfully shy.

"I have to take some cookies home for *Daed*."

"I will remind you." Emma rose to her feet. "Wayne, I want to thank you for this chance to get to know Sophie. I shall take good care of her. I'll bring her home about seven. Is that acceptable?"

"I reckon." He tipped his hat and left.

Sophie went to a kitchen chair and sat down. She turned her pail first one way and then the other.

"Shall we go to the party?" Emma tried to put some eagerness in her voice.

"Okay." Sophie followed her outside but balked at getting in Emma's buggy.

"What's wrong?" Emma bent to her level.

"It's fancy. I can't ride in a fancy buggy. It has the orange sign on the back."

"It is okay for you to ride in my buggy. My church wants us to use the slow-moving-vehicle sign."

Sophie shook her head. "Nope."

It was too cold for Emma and the child to walk all that way. Emma went to the house and searched for a dark piece of cloth to cover the sign. She found one that worked. Sophie studied it for a few seconds and nodded. "Okay, but you can't turn the lights on."

"I won't."

"My *mamm* died last year. *Daed* doesn't like me to talk about her."

"I'm sorry."

"*Daed* says he might marry you. I don't like that."

"If you don't like it, I for sure won't marry him, but you might like me when you get to know me."

"Maybe. Can we go to the party now?"

"Yes, we can and we are going to have a wonderful time."

Luke stood in the corner of the living room, waiting and watching for Emma. Rebecca stopped beside him. "She'll be here."

"Who?" he asked with indifference.

"Emma. You aren't fooling anyone. It's easy to see how you feel about her."

He gathered his nerve. "I do care for Emma but I don't know how she feels about me or about Wayne. Do you?"

"I can ask her."

"I was hoping you'd say that."

She just chuckled as she walked away.

People from his church group and others mingled throughout the house. Children had been relegated to the basement. The downstairs room ran the entire length of the house and was used mainly for parties and singings for the teenagers.

Long tables held goodies in every shape and form from brownies to cookies to cake and pie. People were required to bring a large pail of treats, set them out and then fill up their pail with treats made by someone else. There were several group games in progress downstairs and the noise level was high. Older people sought the comfort of his mother's plush sofa and chairs in the living room. Not caring for crowds, Luke picked a spot where he could watch for Emma without having to visit with people.

He spied her the minute she walked in, but he didn't know the child with her. Was it Wayne's daughter? Or some other relative of Emma's that he didn't know about? He gathered his courage and made his way across the room. He'd soon know if she was still angry with him, but for the moment he was going to take Joshua's advice and act like the kiss hadn't happened. "Evening, Emma. Who have you got with you?"

Her smile looked strained. "This is Sophie Hochstetler. Wayne's daughter. She and I are getting to know each other. Sophie, say hello to Luke."

Sophie buried her face in Emma's skirt. "I can't talk to strangers. They might be shunned."

Emma lifted the child's face. "I know for a fact that Luke is not shunned."

"I don't like him."

"Not many people do," Luke said with a smile, hoping to tease her out of her sour mood. If Emma was getting to know Wayne's daughter, it must be serious between them.

Sophie scowled at him. He smiled at Emma. "This may be a job for Hannah and Bella."

"That's just who I was going to find." Emma looked around the room.

"Basement." He nodded toward the steps.

"Danki." She went downstairs with the child and he didn't see either of them again for over an hour.

Emma finally managed to get Sophie to play with some of the other children. Rather they were playing and Sophie was watching them, but at least she wasn't clinging to Emma's hand.

Rebecca stopped beside her. "How is it going with Sophie?"

"Not great."

"How are things going with Wayne?"

Emma knew she could tell Rebecca the truth. "Not great, either."

"What seems to be the problem?"

"Me."

Rebecca leaned closer. "Care to elaborate on that?"

"When did you know Samuel was the one for you?"

"I realized it when I couldn't fall asleep at night without thinking about him. Who do you fall asleep thinking about?"

Not Wayne. "I don't care to say."

"Someone has asked me to be their go-between."

Emma's pulse jumped up a notch. Was it Luke? "Who asked you?"

"I think you know." Rebecca leaned away with a decided twinkle in her eyes.

"Luke." Emma's excitement dimmed. A growing sense of annoyance settled in her chest. He could have asked her anytime they were together in the store or on the buggy ride to the hardware store or after he'd kissed her in the snow. Why did he feel the need to send a go-between?

Was she that hard to speak with? Did he expect

her to reject him? Scold him? He could kiss her, but he couldn't ask her a simple question.

Emma folded her arms. It wasn't a simple question or she would have an answer for Rebecca at this very moment and she didn't.

"Well?" Rebecca prompted. "What shall I tell him?"

The party was winding down when Luke finally met up with Rebecca. "Have you had a chance to get Emma alone?"

Her smile was forced. "I did."

"She doesn't want to go out with me." His hopes withered on the vine.

"That isn't exactly what she said."

"What did she say?"

"That you're a big boy now and you can ask her yourself."

"That's not bad, is it?"

"It was more in the way she said it."

"I see." So it wasn't good.

"If God wants you to be together, Luke, you will overcome every obstacle. Samuel and I are proof of that."

"At least I didn't get shut down."

Rebecca nodded and walked away. Luke considered his next move. Emma hadn't said no. Was she waiting to say that to his face? He could see her doing that.

He started down the steps to the basement to

locate her. She was easy to spot. He never had trouble picking her out in a crowd. There was just something special about her.

Standing by Mary and Joshua, Emma was encouraging Sophie to pet Bella. It wasn't working. Sophie was afraid of the dog and batted at her if she ventured too close. Hannah came to stand beside him. "I don't like her. She said my dress was too fancy. It's not. *Mammi* Ada made it for me. She doesn't like Bella, either."

"Maybe she's never had a dog."

"That would be sad," Hannah said with a quivering lip.

It would be sad for the motherless child to be fearful of everything including the most lovable mutt in the world. She was blessed to have Emma watching over her. He might selfishly want Emma to choose him over Wayne, but there was more than his feelings at stake. He walked up to Sophie. "Hi, remember me? I'm not shunned."

"Can we go now?"

"How would you like to go down to the river? Have you seen it at night? It's very pretty."

"That's a *goot* idea. I'll get our coats." Emma cast a relieved smile his way, and he knew he'd made the right decision.

When she had the child bundled up, Luke opened the back door, and they walked out to find a young couple smooching on the garden bench. He cleared his throat and the couple sprang apart. It was Noah and their neighbor's daughter, Fannie Erb.

Luke walked past and whispered, "Carry on, bro."

"Will do."

Luke and Emma continued down to the water's edge with the child. Away from the noise and the crush of people, Sophie slowly relaxed. After a few minutes, she looked at Luke. "Can I throw a rock in the water?"

Emma crouched beside her. "You can throw every rock you find in the river. Just don't get too close to the water."

"Danki." She picked up a pebble from a spot free of snow and chucked it in. The ripples spread out, sparkling in the moonlight.

She spun to Emma. "Did you see that?"

"I did. Try throwing two rocks together," Emma suggested.

Sophie became more animated as she tossed stones and ran along the riverbank.

"How did you know she would do better outside?" Emma was looking at him with curiosity.

"You could pick them out in prison, the ones who couldn't tolerate being closed in. She had that look of panic on her face."

"I'm glad you saw it. I was at my wit's end."

Her eyes held a softness he hadn't seen before. Not when she was looking at him. Could he kiss her again? Would she let him? The thought had barely formed when a shriek split the night.

Chapter Thirteen

Emma dashed away from Luke and ran to the water's edge. Sophie, cowering and crying, was backed up against a tree as Bella tried to interest her in a stick. She laid it at the girl's feet and pushed it closer.

Emma picked Sophie up. "It's all right. She won't hurt you. Go away now, Bella."

The dog walked off with her head down. Sophie kept her arms locked around Emma's neck. "I don't like her."

"I'm sorry she scared you." Emma turned to Luke. "I need to take her home."

"I'll drive you." He hurried away to get her horse and buggy hitched.

She walked up the hill with Sophie in her arms. Several people had come out, Isaac and Anna among them. "What happened?" Anna asked.

"Bella scared her."

"Poor Bella wouldn't hurt a fly. What did she do, child?" Anna stroked the girl's cheek.

"She hit me with a stick."

Emma explained. "Bella was trying to give it to her so she would throw it in the water."

Isaac patted his wife's arm. "The dog will fetch right through the ice if she has to. She doesn't care how cold the water is."

Pressing her way through the crowd, Emma murmured her excuses and carried Sophie to the door. She only had to wait for a minute before Luke drove up. Sophie scrambled from her arms into the front seat. She glared at Luke. "I don't want him to come along."

Emma said, "I'll drive, Luke. Thanks for the offer."

"Are you sure?"

"We'll be fine, won't we, Sophie?"

"I want to go home now."

Luke handed Emma up into the driver's seat. She grasped his hand. "*Danki*. I appreciate all your help."

"Anytime."

Hannah came running out with Sophie's pail. It was filled with cookies. "Don't forget this. I'm sorry you didn't like my dog."

Sophie didn't answer. Emma set her horse in motion and drove Sophie to her father's farm. Wayne came out when they pulled up. "How was the party?"

"I didn't like it. They had a dog that scared me, but Emma chased it away. She's nice. I brought you some cookies." He lifted her out of the buggy.

Emma gave him a sympathetic smile. "I'm sorry she didn't have a good time. She was frightened by Hannah's dog, but no harm was done."

"Will I see you again?" he asked.

"I'm usually at home." She couldn't in good conscience invite him for a visit, but she hated to disappoint him after her disastrous evening with his daughter.

"I'll stop in one of these days."

"Can I come, too?" Sophie asked.

Emma nodded and turned her horse toward home.

On the Sunday before Christmas, Luke made up his mind to ask Emma if he could court her. He decided to get it over with after church and kill the butterflies in his stomach. Once she said no, he was free to look elsewhere. Not that he would.

If she agreed, it would mean he would have to join the faith. Was he ready for that? He had to be. It was the only way they could be together. This had to be what God wanted for him.

When the long service was over, he stood beside her buggy, waiting for her to come out of the house after the meal had been served. She came up the hill toward him with a basket over her arm. "Hello, Luke."

"Emma, would you like to ride home with me?"

She raised her chin a notch, and he prepared himself for her rejection. She nodded once. "I would."

Had he heard her correctly? "You would?"

"Are you ready to leave now?"

"*Ja. Ja*, we can leave now. Let me get my horse hitched up and tell your brothers you won't be going home with them."

"All right. I'll wait here."

He tripped getting down the hill but recovered without falling. He looked to see if she was watching. She was. She pressed her hand to her lips to hide her smile, but he could see the humor in her eyes.

Hurrying across to the corral, he located his mare and soon had her harnessed to his open cart. He gave thanks for the mild weather as the sunshine warmed his face. Emma wouldn't be uncomfortable riding with him.

She had agreed so readily. He was still amazed. Locating Roy and Alvin in the barn with other boys their age, Luke told the pair he was taking their sister home. Roy never even glanced up from the phone in his hand. "Okay, fine."

So much for opposition from her family. Luke

hurried back outside and skidded to a stop when he saw Emma wasn't by her buggy. Had she changed her mind?

Glancing around, he saw she was standing on the other side of his cart. When his heart started beating again, he walked calmly in her direction. "Are you ready?"

"I am."

Taking the basket from her, he placed it behind the seat, and held out his hand so she could steady herself while getting in. After a second of hesitation, she laid her hand in his. A jolt of pleasure raced up his arm and spread throughout his body. Her cheeks turned pink. Did she feel it, too? He wanted to say something, but nothing came to mind so he walked around the cart and got in.

When he was seated, he glanced her way. "Are you worried about people seeing us together?"

"*Nee*, why should I be?"

"I don't have a spotless reputation."

She fixed her gaze on his. "I'm not concerned about what you did in the past. It's your action now and in the future that truly matters to me."

"Then I'll behave myself."

Arching one eyebrow, she snapped back, "See that you do."

He laughed as he turned the horse and started down the lane. At the highway, he paused. "Shall

I take you directly home, or would you like to take the long way there?"

"The long way should be a very pretty drive today."

Happiness surged through his blood. "The long way it is."

A secondary road split off from the highway a few hundred yards from the lane that followed the curve of the river between the low hills. Luke turned into it, noticing several other sets of tracks in the fresh snow. It was a popular drive for young couples with several secluded places they could turn off and enjoy some privacy. The first two such places already had buggies parked in them, so Luke drove on. He wanted to say something, but Emma's silence had stifled his tongue. She sat beside him, seemingly enjoying the ride. He didn't want to spoil it for her.

He relaxed and began to enjoy the view, too. Snow covered the hillsides in a thick white blanket that sparkled everywhere the sunlight touched it. The trees had long since lost their leaves and their stark branches reached toward the blue sky while their identical shadows intertwined with their neighbors on the snow-covered ground. The river, nearly a solid sheet of ice, gurgled up in open spots before disappearing under the ice again. A dozen Canada geese occupied one section of open water. He gestured toward them with his head. "Think one of them will become someone's Christmas goose?"

"I hope not. They're so pretty. I love to see the flocks in huge Vs traveling across the sky. Sometimes I hear them at night and wonder why they travel in the darkness."

"I reckon because they can tell where they are by the stars or by the rivers heading south below them."

She gazed upward. "It must be a wonderful thing to see the world from so high in the air."

"True, but I think a snug house and a warm fire must beat the view when the weather turns nasty. I'm glad I'm not a goose."

Chuckling, she glanced his way. "So true." She paused. "Father will be so happy that the store can open when he returns."

"He's been really pressing to get it done. Why the rush?"

He glanced at Emma in time to see a look of pain flash across her face before she schooled her features into a calm expression. "He has his reasons."

Luke knew something wasn't right. He pulled the horse to a stop. "Emma, what's wrong? Tell me."

"Nothing. It's nothing."

"It is. I can see you're worried."

"It's nothing that concerns you."

She didn't want to discuss it. Not with him.

It wasn't his concern. His happiness at the day faded. If she couldn't confide in him, then what hope was there for something more between them?

Emma wished with all her heart that she could tell Luke about her father's illness. She needed to talk to someone about it, but her promise to her father kept her silent. She shivered and pulled her cloak tightly across her chest.

"I should get you home. It's too cold for an open buggy ride."

"I'm fine."

"You always say that. Even when you aren't fine. I'm taking you home." He set the horse in motion.

He looked so serious. Had she upset him? It wasn't her intention. She had been thrilled when he asked her to ride home with him. Did he know that? Should she say something? She didn't want to appear forward.

An awkwardness appeared between them and she didn't know how to combat it. She sat in silence until they had almost reached her house. She gave one last try to lighten the mood. "Would you like to come in for some apple cake and coffee?"

He pulled his horse to a stop. A hint of a smile lifted the corner of his mouth. "Apple cake isn't cherry cobbler, but it will do."

She saw her brothers coming out of the barn. They had reached home before her. She had been hoping for some more time alone with Luke. Her spirits plunged lower when she saw Wayne Hochstetler was with them. She wasn't up to a visit with him, but she could hardly send him home.

"Have I come at a bad time?" Wayne eyed her closely. It must look as if she had accepted a ride home from church with Luke, because she had. From the look on Wayne's face, she knew he thought she was behaving poorly by stepping out with Luke, too, but she wasn't dating Wayne. Not yet.

Wayne was her father's choice. She couldn't turn him away. She had promised to consider him and, so far, she had barely given him a chance. He wasn't as fun-loving as Luke, but he was firmly rooted in their community and their church. Something Luke couldn't say.

She forced a cheerful smile for Wayne's benefit. "It's not a bad time at all. I was just offering Luke some apple cake. Would you care for some?"

He smiled for the first time since he had been coming by. "It's a favorite dessert of mine."

"How is your daughter?"

"Fine. She talks about you all the time. About how you and she threw stones in the river, and how you comforted her when the dog scared her.

She likes you a great deal and hopes to see you again soon so she can learn how to make cookies and cakes for me. I didn't realize how much she missed having a woman's company."

"I'm glad I could help. She's a sweet child. Let us go inside."

Roy took hold of Luke's reins. "Do you want me to put her in the barn for you?" he asked hopefully.

Luke shook his head. "I won't be staying that long."

"But you just got here." Roy gave Wayne a sour look.

It didn't faze Wayne. He held out his hand to help Emma down from the open carriage. "You must be cold after riding in this. Luke should have more sense."

Luke's eyes narrowed. Emma spoke quickly. "I'm not cold at all. A ride in the open was very refreshing. *Danki*, Luke, for obliging me."

If that gave Wayne the impression the buggy ride had been her idea, that was fine. She allowed him to help her down. Pulling off her gloves, she stuffed them into the pocket of her cloak. "Come inside."

The glare the two men shared would have been funny if she hadn't been the cause. Feeling like a mouse caught between two tomcats, she strode into the house and took off her cloak and bonnet.

Her brothers, Luke and Wayne came in and hung up their hats and coats.

"Have a seat in the living room, all of you. It will take me a few minutes to get things ready."

They all trouped into the other room. Instead of friendly chatter, Emma heard only silence. That did not bode well for a congenial visit. After making coffee and handing out slices of cake, Emma took a seat in her chair. Everyone ate without speaking.

The minute he had finished his cake, Luke rose. "I have to be going."

"Already?" Yes, Wayne was her father's choice, but Emma was loath to spend an afternoon with him. She was afraid the silence would continue.

Luke turned to Wayne. "It was good to see you again."

Wayne nodded, but he didn't say anything.

Roy rose to his feet quickly. "I'll see you out, Luke." They both left.

The silence was broken by Alvin jumping up. "I'll go see him out, too," he said, and left the room.

Wayne scowled after Alvin. "How many people does it take to show Luke Bowman the door?"

"Apparently, all of us. Excuse me. I forgot to tell him something. I'll be back in a moment."

Emma told herself she wanted to know if Luke would be over the next day, but it was just an excuse to see him again. She opened the door and stepped outside. Luke stood beside his horse, adjusting the headband. "The man has a personality of a toad. An old thick toad."

"Not even a toad. A rock," Roy added.

Alvin punched his brother's shoulder. "More like a stick of wood. Or a thick block of wood between his ears."

Her brothers and Luke all laughed.

Emma marched down the steps. "How dare you make fun of a guest in this house! Alvin, Roy, I'm ashamed of you. And of you, too, Luke Bowman."

She glanced at the house to make sure Wayne hadn't followed her. "It's one thing to have a poor opinion about someone, but don't lead my brothers astray by voicing it in front of them."

Luke flushed a dull red. "I'm sorry, but you have to admit that Wayne doesn't have much of a personality. Come on. Anyone can see that."

"And everyone can see how immature you are when you hold him up to ridicule. You need to grow up, Luke."

"Why does Wayne keep coming over, anyway?" Roy asked.

Emma pressed her lips tightly together. "Your father asked him to look in on us."

"He wants to marry your sister." Luke climbed into his buggy and picked up the reins.

Roy turned stricken eyes to her. "You aren't considering him, are you?"

"He's a stalwart member of our faith. I am considering him," she said loudly, wanting Luke to hear.

He did. His face went blank. "I pray you'll be happy."

Why won't you speak up and tell me how you feel, Luke? You have to know I still care. I let you kiss me. Tell me you're going to stay, join the faith and be happy among us. Don't make me watch you leave again.

Roy took a step away from her. "Even if you marry him, I'm not going to let that toad boss me around."

She whirled to face her brother. "Wayne is not a toad. He's a God-fearing man who has suffered the tragic loss of his wife. He has a daughter who has lost her mother. We know what that feels like, don't we? Where is your sympathy, Roy?"

His expression grew mulish, then the cell phone in his boot rang. He pulled it out. Emma snatched it from his hand and threw it away. "I told you to get rid of that."

Roy raced to pick it up. "I hate you and this whole backward place."

He took off toward the barn with Alvin following him and begging him to wait.

"Emma, that was uncalled for," Luke said quietly.

Everything was so wrong. Her father was dying. Her brother hated her. Luke didn't love her. She couldn't carry it all alone. Her self-control fell into tatters.

"You don't get to tell me what to do, Luke Bowman. You don't have that right."

"Emma, please, I don't want to fight."

"Then you should leave. I don't need you anymore. We can handle things ourselves and I sure don't need you encouraging my brothers to make fun of Wayne or filling Roy's head with ideas about going away to school and working on solar cells. We were better off before you started interfering."

"Don't worry. It'll never happen again." Luke turned his horse and drove out of the yard without another word.

She watched him leave and pressed a hand to her forehead. "Oh, what have I done?"

Luke rode home in a daze with Emma's words echoing in his mind. *I don't need you anymore.*

Hearing them hurt more than he had imagined any words could hurt. Now he knew how badly he must have wounded Emma in the past and he grew sick to his stomach. She had needed him then, and he turned away from her out of shame.

He had been wrong to make fun of Wayne, that was true, but Emma's anger was about more than that. She didn't trust him enough to share her troubles. Without trust, there wasn't anything to build a foundation on. He'd been foolish to dream things might change between them.

It didn't take him long to reach home. He was rubbing down his horse when his father walked into the barn. "Luke, I'm surprised to see you home so soon. Rebecca said you'd be visiting until late today."

"That was the plan. It didn't work out that way."

"Care to talk about what's wrong?"

Luke almost said no, but then stopped himself. It wasn't fair to expect Emma to share her troubles if he was too proud to share his own with his father.

He took a deep breath. "I'm in love with Emma, but she doesn't love me." It was a deeply humbling experience to say it aloud.

"I see." His father came to the stall door and leaned on it. "I'm sorry. You told her how you feel and she told you she didn't feel the same?"

"It wasn't hard to figure out. I don't know why I thought she might care for me."

"The heart is a fierce thing. It will hold on to hope in the face of all evidence to the contrary. It is our mind that tricks us into giving up."

"Or it's our mind that lets us see the truth our hearts don't want to accept."

"I would rather believe my heart. It has stood me in good stead these many years. My mind said you were lost to me forever not so long ago, but my heart never gave up on you."

Luke blinked back the sting of his tears. "I'm sorry for all the pain I caused you and *Mamm*."

"And I am grateful to *Gott* that He brought you back to us. Maybe you should tell Emma what is in your heart and not let your brain have the final say."

"It's too late for that."

"As you will. Seek the council of our Heavenly Father in this matter. He knows the secrets of every heart."

Luke nodded but didn't speak. His head and his heart were telling him it was over with Emma.

Could he stay in Bowmans Crossing if she married someone else?

No, he couldn't bear to see her with another. He couldn't live with that kind of torture.

At last he had the answer to his question. When he was free, he would go. He couldn't stay. He wasn't strong enough.

"I may have overreacted." Emma sat across from Rebecca in her living room two days after her disastrous afternoon with Luke. Rebecca had stopped by with a coffee cake and the two were enjoying a late breakfast. At least Rebecca was enjoying it. Emma couldn't swallow a bite.

"In what way?" Rebecca took a sip of coffee.

"I accused Luke of encouraging Roy to poke fun at Wayne. I felt so sorry for Wayne and his daughter. Roy looks up to Luke. Anything Luke says, Roy takes to heart. I yelled at Roy and I threw his phone down and broke it. I yelled at Luke, too. I wasn't a nice person." She needed to apologize to him soon.

"Why do you keep pushing Luke away, when you are clearly in love with him, Emma? It's as plain as the nose on your face. You've loved him for years."

Emma wanted to deny it but she couldn't. She was in love with Luke. "What am I going to do?"

"You know you can't keep stringing Wayne along. You have to tell him how you feel about someone else. You don't have to say it's Luke."

"I don't want to hurt Wayne."

"You could marry Wayne and be miserable for the rest of your life."

"Not such a good option when you put it that way. Do you really think Luke is in love with me? I'm not convinced. He hasn't spoken of it. He hasn't made a move to join the church. What if he intends to leave again?" How could she bear that?

Rebecca finished her coffee and stood. "I've got to get going. Luke will convince you in his own time. Give him some encouragement. Give him a chance."

"How many does he deserve?"

"As many as God gives all of us. When will your father be home?"

"Tomorrow."

"In time to see Alvin in the school Christmas program?"

"Of course."

"Then I shall see him there. Be of good cheer, Emma. It will all work out as God wills. I've got to run the rest of the costumes up to the school and get busy baking. I can't believe Christmas is almost here."

After saying goodbye to Rebecca, Emma went out to the new hardware store half-filled with items waiting to be sold. Alvin was stocking the shelves from his boxes. At least this project had gone right.

She looked around for Roy. "Alvin, where is your brother?"

"I haven't seen him. I think he's still in his room. Do you realize we missed his birthday yesterday?"

Emma slapped her hands to her cheeks. "I forgot. How could I forget? No wonder he is staying out of sight. I'll go up and apologize."

She climbed the stairs and knocked on his door. There was no answer. She opened it and stopped in the doorway. The room was empty. The bed neatly made. His clothes were gone from the pegs on his wall. His dresser drawers were open and empty as well. Checking under the bed confirmed her worst fears. His suitcase was missing. She turned and raced downstairs.

Luke was almost done packing when there was a knock at his door. He hesitated to speak to anyone, but he said, "Come in."

Samuel looked in. "We missed you at breakfast. Are you sick?"

"I'm fine."

"Tomorrow is the big day. Last parole visit. You'll be a free man."

"Yup."

"So why are you packing now? And why are you packing so much?"

"Jim and I are going to Cincinnati a day early."

"You've got more than two days' worth of clothes in that bag."

Luke stopped what he was doing. This was so hard. "That's because I'm not coming back."

"That was my next guess. Are you sure about this?"

Emma was considering marrying a man with a daughter who needed her. Luke couldn't compete with that. He was nothing but an ex-con and an ex-junkie. "I'm sure. I'll write this time."

"Can't you wait until after Christmas to leave? For the family?"

A honk outside told him Jim was waiting. "Nobody is going to be shocked by this." He zipped his bag shut and headed for the door.

"You're wrong about that. We all thought you would stay."

"Sorry to disappoint you again. Goodbye."

Chapter Fourteen

"What do you mean our brother is missing?" Alvin frowned at Emma.

"Missing. As in not here. His clothes are gone along with the money I know he keeps in an envelope taped under his bedside table."

Emma was already moving toward the kitchen as a sickening sensation churned in her midsection.

Alvin grabbed her arm. "He wouldn't do this."

Shouting for Roy, Alvin charged up the steps. There was no answer.

Emma folded her arms tightly across her middle. How could he do this when she needed his support more than ever?

Unable to accept that his headstrong brother had abandoned them, Alvin flew down the stairs and raced out the front door. Standing on the front porch, he shouted Roy's name into the whirling snow and then raced to the barn.

Emma sat at the table with her head in her hands. After a few minutes, she felt Alvin's hand on her arm. "He wants to live *Englisch*. I reckon he decided it was time."

"Not now. Not at Christmas. Not with our father ill. How could Roy do this to us?" Emma realized she was wringing her hands. She crossed her arms and tucked her cold fingers beneath her armpits.

"I thought *Daed* was better."

She stared into Alvin's worry-filled eyes. This wasn't the time to share what she knew about their father's condition. "He doesn't want us fretting about him, you know that. He is in God's hands, and *Gott es goot. Ja?*"

"*Ja.* Do you think God will bring Roy back? I mean, Luke came back."

"Roy will come to his senses. I'm sure of it." Only she wasn't. If only she could talk to Roy and make him understand how much she needed him, how sorry she was.

Was Luke right? In her struggle to manage the business and the home, had she pushed Roy aside, making him feel like a troublesome child instead of the man of the family?

Alvin turned back toward the front door. "Luke will be here soon. He'll know what we should do."

Her heart sank. "I'm afraid Luke isn't coming today."

Alvin scowled at her. "Why not?"

Emma walked to the kitchen window and looked out. "We had a disagreement. I told him we didn't need him anymore. We don't. We'll be fine."

"Are you crazy? How could you tell him we didn't need him? We do. We've only got half the inventory priced and on the shelves."

"He's not dependable."

"I love you, sister, but you can be every bit as willful and stubborn as Roy. This isn't the time to be prideful."

"I'm not prideful."

"You're not forgiving, either. We need Luke."

"Let's worry about your brother. Where do you think he would go?"

"To the city."

Tears filled her eyes. She threw her arms around Alvin and pulled him close. "*Nee*, he wouldn't do that. Not now."

Alvin pulled away. "I hear a buggy. Maybe it's Luke." He shot out the front door.

Maybe it was Roy returning. Had he taken the buggy? She hadn't checked. She snatched her coat from the peg and ran out after Alvin.

It wasn't Luke or Roy. Wayne stepped down from his buggy. She rushed to his side. "Wayne, I'm so glad to see you. Roy has run away. What should I do?"

"Are you certain? Maybe he is staying with one of his friends."

"He's taken all his clothes. Can you take me to the bus station? I'm not sure when the next bus leaves. He might still be there."

"*Nee*, Emma. You must not seek him out. If he has left the faith, then you must shun him until he repents and returns of his own accord."

"He's only a boy, Wayne. He's not been baptized."

"Then according to your ways, he is free to go. Our Creator endowed all men with free will."

"Yes, he's free to go, but he has no idea what is waiting for him out there."

"I will pray that he learns the error of his ways and comes home a humbled man. I need two number-0 horseshoes. Do you carry them?"

"You can ask me about horseshoes when my brother is missing?" She stared at him in horror.

"Emma, your brother made his choice."

"And I have made mine. We will not suit. I will not go out with you. I wish you well."

"I'm sorry to have wasted my time."

"As am I. You will find horse supplies in the back of the store. Take what you need and leave the money under the counter. Alvin, get a horse hitched. We'll go after Roy ourselves."

He ran to do as she asked. She jumped in when he came out of the barn, took the reins and put her horse into a fast trot. Twenty minutes later, she pulled her tired horse to a stop beside the filling station that doubled as a bus stop. She handed the reins to Alvin. "Walk him to cool him down and keep an eye out for Roy. I'll check the bus schedule."

Hopping down from the buggy, she hurried inside. The man behind the counter was helpful and used to seeing Amish kids heading off on their own.

"I knew as soon as I saw him he was a runaway. They have that look about them. Scared and trying to look bold at the same time. Your brother, you say?" He leafed through his ticket book.

"He's only seventeen." Just a baby. She bit her lip to keep from crying.

"Here it is."

"I'll take a ticket for one to wherever he went."

"He purchased a ticket to Columbus with a transfer to Cincinnati at four-thirty last evening. The line makes a lot of stops. If he stayed on the bus, he would have arrived in Cincinnati by one in the morning."

"Cincinnati? Oh, Roy, what have you done?" Her plan to follow him vanished like her breath on a cold windy day. Even if she followed him, how would she find him among the thousands of people there?

"Do you still want a ticket? The next bus

taking the same route doesn't leave until four-thirty in the afternoon on Christmas Eve."

She shook her head. "*Nee*, but thank you."

Roy was gone. Would she ever see him again? She walked slowly outside.

Alvin drew the buggy to a stop beside her. "I didn't see him. Did you find out if he's left?"

"He has gone to Cincinnati."

Worry filled Alvin's eyes. "What does that mean?"

"It means your brother is *Englisch* now."

"But he'll come home, right? Emma, he'll be home soon."

"I don't know."

"We should talk to Luke. He'll know what to do."

It was so tempting, but no. She hardened her heart. "*Nee*, this is our business and none of his."

"Roy wouldn't miss Christmas with us. He'll be back for Christmas. I know it."

She prayed Alvin was right. "Let's go home. You must get to school. God will deliver Roy to us. We will pray and we will have faith."

Emma drove Alvin to school in a state of shock. Her mind had stopped functioning. After dropping her brother at school, she drove home. Only the echoes of the empty house greeted her when she walked in. How could Roy do this? If she had told him about his father, would it have made a difference? There was no way to know. She was simply second-guessing herself now.

Her father's letter said he would be home about noon tomorrow. More than anything, she dreaded giving him this news.

Did Luke know? Had he helped Roy escape a life he didn't want? Luke knew how to do it. She longed to throw herself in Luke's arms and beg his forgiveness. She needed his strength and comfort. Tears slipped down her cheeks. She had driven Luke and Roy away. Her pride was cold comfort now.

That night she didn't sleep at all. Instead, she paced her bedroom floor, stopping every few minutes to look out into the night. Hoping and praying her brother would return. She saw only darkness beyond her windowpane. When the sky grew light again just before dawn, Emma fell to her knees at the window. It was Christmas Eve morning.

"Please, God, show me what to do. Keep Roy safe. That's all I ask."

She closed her eyes in prayer and Luke's face appeared to her, his eyes full of pain at her cruel words. Her fear of being abandoned again had caused her to push away the man she loved. The one man who could help her now.

She needed Luke, not just to help find Roy but to make her life complete. She had to tell him. She wouldn't let one more chance pass her by.

When Alvin came down to breakfast, she could tell he hadn't slept, either. "I don't want to go to school."

"I know, but your classmates and Teacher Lillian are depending on you. There is so much that still needs to be done."

"How can I sing with Roy gone? I don't want to."

"*Daed* will be home today. You want him to hear you sing, don't you?"

"Knowing Roy is gone will break his heart."

That was what she feared, too. "Your songs will give him comfort, Alvin. I think you should go to school."

"What are you going to do?"

"I'm going to ask Luke to help us. I'm praying he knows where Roy might have gone."

Alvin threw his arms around her. "*Danki.* He'll know how to get Roy back. You'll see."

She patted her brother's back. "I know he will. The bus leaves this afternoon, so I won't get to see your program tonight."

"That's okay. Roy is more important. What do we tell *Daed*?"

"The truth. He'll be home around noon. I'll go to see Luke as soon as I've explained things to *Daed*."

Alvin reluctantly left for school. Emma worked in the shop until she heard a car pull in a little after nine. She walked slowly to the door, dreading the coming reunion.

Luke walked out the door of the parole office and stopped in the bright winter sunshine. The early-morning air was cold and tainted with the smell of car exhaust, but he breathed in deeply. *I'm free. It's over.*

"What now?" Jim stood waiting for him at the bottom of the steps. He glanced at his watch. "It's half past nine. Want to get in a little shopping before we head home?"

"Take me to the bus station."

Jim's smile faded. "Let me drive you home, Luke. That's where you belong."

What was the point of going back? Emma would never be his. He didn't deserve her, anyway. He'd done his time. He was a free man. Free to go anywhere and do anything except the one thing he wanted to do more than he wanted to draw his next breath. To tell Emma he loved her. To hold her in his arms and never let her go. But it would be another man who held her. Another man would care for her, give her children and grow old beside her.

A black hole of despair opened in front of him. Facing a life without her was impossible. He wanted to forget his burning need for her. He needed to forget. And he knew exactly how he could make that happen.

"There is a motel called the Gray Cat a few blocks from the bus depot. If you can drop me there, that's all I need. That and some time to think things over."

"I wish you'd change your mind."

Luke shook his head. Jim walked ahead of him to the car and drove him to his destination without another word until he pulled into the parking lot of the motel. He turned in his seat to look at Luke. "Don't do something stupid."

"I won't." He smiled at his friend. Something stupid had been thinking that he could have a life with Emma. She had been the smart one this time.

He got out of the car and went to check in. The three-story building was old and smelled of the unwashed occupants that frequented it. It was cheap, and the owner had friends in low places. He was the man Luke needed to see. He stopped in front of the desk. Behind the wire mesh, a woman in a tight minidress with pale purple hair was filing her nails.

"Can I get a room?"

She looked up and her eyes widened. "Luke Bowman, is that you?"

It took him a second to realize he was facing the woman who had testified against him and wrongfully imprisoned his brother Joshua. Time had not been kind to her. She looked ten years older instead of three. "Hello, Maggie."

"I sure never thought I'd see you again. So you got out."

"No thanks to you."

Her eyes hardened. "A girl has to do what a girl has to do. I was looking at a long stretch. It was my third arrest. The DA offered me a deal if I rolled on you and your brother. What choice did I have?"

"You had a choice. You could've told the truth. My brother had nothing to do with the drugs I was moving for you."

"Don't be like that. He got out early, didn't he? I'm sure he's back on the farm, milking cows and growing corn. You Amish boys are a funny bunch. You race here to live it up and go crying home when life gets hard. I had another one come in yesterday. What a dope. He thinks I'm the hottest thing since horseshoes."

"I hope he comes to his senses long before I did."

She moved to the door at the side of her desk, unlocked it and came out to stand beside Luke. "We can let bygones be bygones, can't we, Luke? You kept your mouth shut about my operation, and I appreciated that. I always liked you."

She placed her fingers on his arm, walked them up to his shoulder and slipped them into his hair at the nape of his neck. "I've got some good stuff at my place. I'll share. It won't even cost you."

It was what he wanted, wasn't it? This was why he'd come here. To forget. To close his eyes and slip into that sweet stupor that made everything tolerable. His body trembled at the thought of it.

God help me. What am I doing?

Emma's face appeared before his mind's eye, followed by his mother and father. He was free now. Free to go where he wanted. Free to live a worthy and decent life.

Forgetting Emma was impossible. It would be hard to see her married to another if she chose that path, but it would be harder still to have her know he had fallen so low again. Seeing her happy would be enough for him.

Newfound warmth spread through his body. He didn't have to do this alone. God was standing beside him, offering His comfort and His strength when Luke's failed.

He lifted Maggie's arms from his neck. "I've changed my mind about a room."

"You're welcome to stay with me. I'm on my own at the moment."

"None of us are really alone, Maggie. God is with us always. I forgive you for the lies you told about me and my brother. I pray you find the peace that I have now."

"Well, la-di-da. You got religion, did you? Take it someplace else. My clientele won't appreciate it." She turned her back on him and reentered her cage, snapping the door shut behind her.

He left the building and walked outside with a light heart. He didn't have to be a slave to drugs. He was free. It would always be a struggle, but for the first time he believed it was a battle he could win with God's help.

He didn't have to return to Bowman's Crossing. It might be easier for Emma if he didn't, but he would visit his family often. The solar installation school he had read about was here in the city. Maybe he should start there.

After he got a letter off to his family letting them know his plans.

To Luke's surprise, Jim Morgan was still sitting in his car at the curb. His face lit up in a bright smile when he caught sight of Luke. With a casualness that belied his racing heart, Luke opened the passenger's side door and slid in the front seat.

Jim pounded Luke's shoulder with his fist. "I knew you didn't belong here. Thank God you realized it. It's really a merry Christmas Eve now. Buckle up. I know exactly where to go to celebrate."

Emma's father sat at the kitchen table nursing a cup of coffee. Emma sat across from him waiting for him to speak.

He looked up with bloodshot eyes. There were

still traces of tears on his cheeks. He'd lost more weight while he was gone. Her heart ached for him.

He pushed his coffee aside. "Wayne is right. We'll have to pray Roy comes home. That's all we can do. He has to come home on his own."

"I'll pray but I'll look, too. I have to try."

"It should be me going to Luke."

"You're tired. You've had a long journey. You need to rest up. Alvin is looking forward to you watching his school program and hearing him sing. It's all he has talked about since you've been gone. You can't disappoint him."

"You should be there, too."

"I will be. In spirit. Lie down for a little while." She glanced at the clock. It was almost eleven. She helped her father to his room, saw him settled and then raced out the door on foot. Her father would need their buggy later.

It took her twenty minutes to reach the river. She was out of breath but once she entered the covered bridge, she got her second wind and ran all the way to the Bowmans' front door. Breathing heavily and worried about what Luke would say to her, she knocked on the door, then pressed a hand to her pounding heart.

She looked up when the door opened, but it was Samuel. "Emma, what's wrong?"

"I must speak to Luke. It's terribly important."

"I'm afraid Luke is gone."

She closed her eyes. "I forgot about his parole meeting. When will he be back?"

"He's not coming back."

Her eyes flew open and she saw the sadness etched on Samuel's face. Her blood turned cold and stopped flowing. "I don't understand."

"Luke has gone back to his *Englisch* life in the city."

"He can't be gone. I need him." A loud buzzing filled her brain. She watched in stunned surprise as the ground rushed toward her face.

Emma, Emma, Emma. The tires on the road hummed her name as Jim's car flew along. Luke's friend hadn't stopped for the past two hours. It turned out the place Jim decided Luke should celebrate Christmas Eve was in Bowmans Crossing. Luke hadn't protested once since he figured out what Jim was up to. Home was where he wanted to be on his first night as a truly free man. A move and a new career could wait until after the holidays.

Leaning back in the seat, he drummed his fingers on the armrest in time with the tires.

"Are you thinking about Emma?" Jim glanced toward Luke.

"All the time, it seems."

"What's going to happen with the two of you?"

"Nothing. If she is happy, that's all I need. I wish I were the man who could make her happy, but it wasn't meant to be. It seems God has other plans for my life and for hers."

"You'll see her tonight. She's not going to miss the school program and neither should you."

"I'm going. I promised Hannah I would be there. Thanks for making me keep that promise. You are welcome to join us."

"Thanks, but no thanks. I've got an aunt in Millersburg who is expecting us for dinner. As soon as I drop you off, I'm collecting Brian and we are on our way."

"It's good to have family close, isn't it?"

"You've never met my aunt or tasted her cooking. We're grabbing a bucket of fried chicken on the way."

As Jim sped on toward Bowmans Crossing, Luke couldn't get his mind off Emma. He realized he wouldn't be able to do that until he had the chance to tell her exactly how he felt about her.

He loved her. He always had and always would.

If she didn't want him, he would bow out of the way. He'd go to school and afterwards he would return to work with his family and try to live a good Amish life. One centered around his faith and his family. It was amazing how those simple words filled his heart and his mind. Once the plain way of life had seemed like a trap. Now it felt safe and welcoming.

It was almost noon by the time Jim dropped Luke at his own front door. He stood outside looking at his home and tried to imagine the shock on Samuel's face and the joy on his mother's when they saw him. He had a lot of apologizing to do.

He pushed open the door and saw the kitchen was empty. He heard the sound of voices and followed them to the living room. Stepping inside, he realized his entire family was gathered there. Samuel saw him first. His eyes widened in astonishment. "Luke, you're back."

"Bad pennies always do that, right?" He set his suitcase down.

His mother gave a glad cry and rushed to throw her arms around him. He held her tight, savoring the smell of cookies that clung to her. "I'm so sorry for the hurt I caused you. I'm home for good, *mudder*," he told her softly. "I will take my vows as soon as possible. I have found forgiveness in God's grace."

She drew back and cupped his face with her hands. "I see that in your eyes. Welcome home. Emma arrived a short time ago. She needs you."

Rebecca and Mary stepped aside and he saw Emma lying on the sofa. He rushed to her and dropped to his knees, taking her cold hand between his own. There were tears on her face. "Darling, what's wrong?"

"Oh, Luke, Roy has run away. Can you find him? Do you know where he's gone?"

Chapter Fifteen

Luke was here. God be praised. Emma held her breath as she waited for him to answer her question. He shook his head. "I don't have any idea where Roy could be. He didn't confide in me."

She closed her eyes against her pain and disappointment. "When I heard you were gone, too, I thought maybe he was with you."

"How long has he been missing?"

"Since the night before last. Help me sit up."

He did, his face a mask of worry. "Are you ill?"

She shook her head. "I was so worried I forgot to eat and the shock of hearing you were gone, too…I guess I fainted."

"You scared me out of a year's growth," Samuel said without malice.

She tried to smile, but failed. "I'm sorry."

"Don't be," Luke said, slipping his arm around her as he sat beside her.

She looked into his beautiful eyes. "Did I hear correctly? Did you say you plan to take your vows?"

"I did."

"You called me darling."

"You had better get used to it. Unless you don't welcome my attention. If that is the case, I apologize."

She cupped his cheek. "I find I do welcome your attention."

"That's the sweetest thing you have ever said to me."

There were a hundred sweet things she wanted to say to him, but all she could think about was her brother. "Have you any idea where Roy might go?"

"None. Do you think he might have hitched a ride out of town?"

"He took the bus. He purchased a ticket to Columbus and then on to Cincinnati. Does that help?"

"It helps a great deal. At least I know where to start looking. Noah, can I use your phone? I need to hire a car to take me to Cincinnati."

"I'm coming with you." She wasn't going to wait at home. She couldn't.

Luke looked as if he would object, but then he slowly nodded. "If you feel well enough."

She turned to Luke's mother. "Anna, if I could have a cup of tea, I would be very grateful."

For the next half hour, Emma sipped her tea and ate a thick ham sandwich while Luke tried to find someone to drive them to the city. He drew a blank on every person the family knew who provided rides for the Amish. Timothy had gone to her father and filled him in on what was happening.

"We can try Nick," Mary suggested. "I know he'll do it for me."

"Might as well try." Luke dialed the number of the sheriff's office and spoke briefly with some-one on the other end. He hung up and looked at Emma. "Nick is tied up at an injury traffic ac-cident. He can't get away."

"What about Jim?" Emma asked.

"He's on his way to Millersburg. But…"

"But what?" she demanded.

He tipped his head to the side. "I know where he keeps the spare keys to his old Jeep. Are you still afraid to ride with me?"

"*Ja*, but I'm coming, anyway."

He smiled and her heart grew light. "That's my girl."

If only she could be.

"I'd better call Jim and tell him my plan." He started to dial the number, but ended up shaking the phone. "Noah, your battery is dead."

Noah took his phone back. "I meant to charge it last night and forgot. I'll hitch up the buggy and drive you to the Morgan place. I can use the phone at the booth to contact Jim after I drop you off."

It only took a few minutes for Noah to bring the buggy around. Luke's father, who had remained quietly beside his wife, spoke up as Emma and Luke got in. "Be careful, *sohn*. Are you breaking the law by doing this?"

Luke gave him a thin smile. "I have a driver's license somewhere. I'm pretty sure Jim will say it's okay for me to borrow the car, so it isn't stealing. If I get pulled over, I'll have a lot of explaining to do, but I don't think I'll go back to jail."

How could she ask Luke to jeopardize his freedom? Emma bit her lower lip. "Is it worth the risk?"

Luke squeezed her hand. "For Roy, *ja*, it is."

Noah drove them to Jim's place. Luke found the key and the old green Jeep roared to life. Emma got in the front seat.

Noah opened Luke's door and took Luke's straw hat, replacing it with his ball cap. "You'll be less likely to get stopped if you don't look like an Amish dude driving a stolen car."

"Danki."

Within a few minutes, they were driving down the highway. Emma watched the scenery flying past. "Do you think we can find him?"

"Maybe. It's a big city, and it's easy to simply disappear. I did for a while."

Emma looked toward him. She had to know

why he'd left. "Did you ever think about me after you were gone?"

Luke's stomach lurched. How could he explain? That episode of his life contained all the shameful things that he had done. More than she knew. How could he make her understand that she—that her memory—had saved him?

"Did I think about you? Only every day."

He glanced her way, but she kept her eyes down, refusing to look at him. "How can I believe that? You never wrote. Not once."

"I wanted you to forget me. I thought it was easier that way."

Her gaze shot to his. "Forget you? You wanted me to forget you? Luke, I fell in love with you when I was twelve. I had been in love with you for years. I was just waiting to grow up so we could marry. And you thought I could forget about you? Why? Because my love couldn't have been real? No, you made it clear how much you cared about me. I was nothing to you. The big wild world beyond Bowmans Crossing was what you loved."

"You're wrong, Emma. I did love you."

"You had a dreadful way of showing it." Her voice was ice-cold.

He gripped the steering wheel even harder. "Don't you see? I did it for you. You belonged in Bowmans Crossing. I never did."

"I belonged with you. Or at least that was what I believed when I was young and foolish. I cried myself to sleep every night for a year. I prayed every night that you would come back. Then I heard you were in prison. I prayed for a letter, a word, anything. Why would a person do that to someone they love? Then I realized I knew the answer. You never loved me. I was a fool."

"Emma, I'm sorry."

She wrapped her arms around herself. "Then don't tell me you thought of me every day."

He wanted to take her in his arms. "I did think of you. I believed that leaving you behind was the only unselfish, honorable thing I ever did in my life. Will you listen to me? Will you hear my story?"

"What can you say that will undo all my pain?"

"Nothing. I hurt you and I'm so, so sorry."

"Was there someone else?"

"*Nee.* There was never anyone but you. But from the time I was little, I knew I didn't belong. I didn't fit in. Samuel was the best possible son. I was the worst possible son. Samuel could do no wrong, and I could do no right. Even when my other brothers came along, that didn't change. I think I hated Samuel as much as I loved him."

"Siblings don't always get along," she said quietly, and he knew she was thinking about Roy.

"Most of the tension was my fault. I couldn't

get *Daed*'s attention by being better at anything, so I got his attention by being a problem. Samuel never wanted anything but to work beside our father and take care of the family. I didn't have the gift for woodworking that they shared. I wanted to know how things worked. I wanted to see what made a machine work. I wanted to understand how men used machines to alter the world. I knew I was going to leave the Amish as soon as I was old enough, but then I noticed you."

She looked out the window. "We've known each other since we were toddlers. We went to the same school for eight years. What do you mean you noticed me?"

He chuckled. "It was during the Christmas play our last year at school. Do you remember it?"

"Of course. It was the highlight of my eighth-grade year. You played a miser without family or friends and I was a poor widow begging shelter on Christmas night."

"I don't remember your lines, only the way you looked at me when you begged me to let you come in out of the storm."

"'Kind sir, you know me not, but I am a cold and hungry widow. Can you not spare a crumb of bread on this feast day?'"

"That was it. I turned you away, but the look in your eyes stayed with me long after the play was done."

"I must have played the part of a cold, hungry widow very well."

He laughed. "Your eyes were green daggers of loathing."

"For your character's actions, not for you."

"So you say now."

"All right, maybe I was upset with you."

"I've always wondered why."

"Because you had asked Mae Beth Shetler if you could walk her home after the singing the week before."

"She turned me down."

"Because she knew I liked you."

"I did ask to drive you home at the next singing."

"It was about time. But I couldn't make you stay when it mattered, could I?" She turned her gaze on him again.

"None of what happened was your fault. Samuel and I had one of our big rows."

"You told me about it when you came over that night. You said you had decided to leave for good."

"And you surprised the life out of me when you said you wanted to come with me."

"I thought you were happy about it."

"I was."

She stared at her clasped hands. "But several nights later you had changed your mind. You didn't want me."

"I wanted you more than ever, but I truly believed I was doing the right thing by sending you home. Samuel caught me as I was sneaking out one night. We had another argument, but I never told you the whole truth about that night. I threw it in Samuel's face that you were going with me. I didn't know it for sure, but I hoped it was true. I just wanted to impress him, to prove someone loved me for who I was. He said my going was the best thing that could happen to our family, but I was ruining your life by taking you with me. He told me your mother was ill. He knew your family was going to need you."

Her head snapped up. "He knew? How did he know? I didn't learn of it until weeks later."

"Your mother came into the shop to ask about having a casket made. She didn't want your father to be burdened with the details."

"That is so like her. She was always looking out for him."

"I was arrested for the first time shortly after that. When I got probation I was too ashamed to go home. Jim took me to the bus station and you know the rest. That was why I left without you. Because Samuel was right. Your family needed you."

"My father is ill. Samuel will be making his casket in a year or two."

"Oh, Emma. I'm so sorry. I didn't know."

"He didn't want the boys to learn of it until

after Christmas. You've seen how excited Alvin is about his school pageant and his solo. *Daed* didn't want to spoil it for him."

"I can understand that."

"Why didn't you write if you cared for me?"

"I wrote you a hundred letters, but I never mailed them. I thought I was ready for the *Englisch* world. I was a naive fool. I couldn't get a job. I didn't have a social security number or a birth certificate. I was too proud to go home. I met someone, a woman. Her name was Maggie."

"Did you love her?"

"It wasn't like that. She said she could help me. I only had to deliver packages for her. I didn't know it was drugs until later. When I found out, she told me it was the only way she could earn enough money to pay for her baby's medical care. She told me he was in the hospital and needed surgery. I believed her and I delivered the packages. She invited me to a party afterward and paid me handsomely. It was easy money and I discovered that drugs made a lonely, scared country boy feel as if he owned the world."

"That still doesn't explain why you didn't write to me. You knew my mother was dying. You knew I would need someone to talk to."

"I'm not making any excuses for what I did. God gave me several chances to turn myself around, but I didn't. It wasn't something I wanted to put on a postcard and mail home. How could

I admit what a failure I was? You know the rest of the story. Joshua came to try and talk some sense into me. He was caught up in a drug raid. Maggie told them that he and I had been making and delivering drugs for months."

"Why did she lie about Joshua's involvement?"

He shrugged. "To save her own hide. She cut a deal for a lesser sentence. Turns out she didn't have a kid. It was all a lie."

"Thank you for telling me this." Emma turned her face to the window again, and he wondered if he had lost her forever by telling the truth.

Emma jolted upright when the car came to a stop. She blinked and rubbed her eyes. "Did I fall asleep?"

"I think so. We're in the outskirts of the city."

There were houses as far as she could see. Soon, the buildings towered over them as they drove along. People streamed along the sidewalk, and cars clogged the road. Hope dwindled in her heart. "How will we ever find him?"

"Don't give up now. I told Roy about a place where I stayed when I first came here."

"You think Roy would go there?"

He turned onto a quieter side street. "Maybe. It's a cheap motel not far from the bus station. I mentioned that a number of runaway Amish kids end up living there. It's a very bad neighborhood.

I tried to get that across to Roy, but I'm not sure it sank in."

She stretched her stiff muscles. The houses had given way to high-rises and now the high-rises gave way to brick buildings with boarded-over windows. The people here weren't hurrying along. They sat on stoops and lounged on car hoods.

"That's it up ahead." Luke pulled the car to a stop. "I want you to wait here, Emma. You will attract too much attention in that garb."

"I am who I am. I won't hide or pretend otherwise. I'm coming with you."

"Then stay close to me."

She didn't argue with that suggestion. Together, they walked along the cracked sidewalk until they reached the parking lot of the motel. Emma heard the sound of a basketball being dribbled in the alley. Roy loved basketball. She caught Luke's sleeve.

He nodded. "We can check it out."

They followed the narrow walkway until it widened into a flat semicircle between three buildings. Someone had put up a makeshift goal. Roy and three other boys were shooting hoops. A woman with purple hair lounged on a chair that held open the back door of the motel. She cheered the boys on.

She caught sight of Luke and frowned. "What are you doing here?"

"Just looking for a friend, Maggie. Roy, can we speak to you?"

Maggie rose to her feet. "He's working for me now, Luke. You should move along before I make trouble."

"Maggie, I know a few good cops these days. My brother married the daughter of a sheriff, did you know that? If I were to tell him where you keep your good stuff stashed and maybe name some of your contacts, like your supplier, how long do you think you'd get this time?"

Her eyes narrowed. "You wouldn't. The Amish don't do things that way."

He simply smiled. "Roy is coming with us."

Emma ignored them. She couldn't take her eyes off Roy. He was all right. Luke had found him.

Roy bounced the ball to one of the other boys and came toward Emma. "I'm not going back. You can't make me."

She pressed a hand to her mouth, then said, "What if I ask nicely?"

Luke laid a hand on Roy's shoulder. "Roy, your sister needs you."

"Emma doesn't need anyone."

She came to stand beside him. "That's where you're wrong, *brudder*. I may act as if I don't need anyone, but that's all it is—an act."

She gazed at Luke, willing him to understand that she was speaking to him as well as Roy. "I know now that I can't do it alone. I need my family. I need my friends, my dearest friends, to understand how frightened I am every single day."

Roy half turned toward her. "Why are you scared?"

She reached out to stroke his hair. "I'm afraid I will do the wrong thing or say the wrong thing and I'll lose what is most precious to me."

Tears blurred her vision, but she saw Luke watching her. What she had to say was for him, too. "A long time ago, I was very much in love with a young man. He left our community, and I thought it was my fault. I mistakenly believed he saw my love as a weakness, as a chain that would bind him when he wanted his freedom. He broke my heart. Afterward, I grew determined to never show that weakness again."

"Love isn't weakness, Emma. Your young man was a fool." Luke walked back to the car, leaving Emma alone with her brother.

"It was Luke, wasn't it?" Roy asked with more perception that she gave him credit for.

"*Ja*, it was Luke, but that is all in the past. Now it's about you. I understand your desire for freedom, Roy. I do. I want you to come home, but if you can't, I will accept that. All I ask is that you forgive me."

"For what?"

"For failing to see what a fine young man you have become. I was afraid of losing my little brother, the one with the runny nose and skinned knees who came crying to me when he got hurt. I wanted to be needed by you, but I could see that you were outgrowing me. I couldn't accept that, so I tried to keep you little. I treated you as the child I wanted you to be. I should have treated you like a man. Can you forgive me?"

"I never really wanted to leave."

"You didn't?" She wanted to hold him close.

"I only did it for Micah."

Puzzled, she shook her head. "I don't understand. I thought it was because you didn't want me to marry Wayne."

"I don't like Wayne, but he wasn't the real reason I left. Micah was the one who wanted to get away. He hated being Amish. He couldn't wait to leave. We talked about it all the time. He had all these big plans. He made me promise to go with him. We were going to go the day after my seventeenth birthday. When he died, I knew I had to follow through on my part. To honor him and what he wanted. What we had planned to do together."

"I can't believe Micah would want you to do this by yourself."

"I miss him so much."

Emma's heart ached for his pain. "I know you do. If you weren't all grown up, I would give you a hug."

"Maybe I'm not that grown up."

She cupped his face with her hands. "You are, but I won't tell anyone if you don't."

"Okay."

She pulled him close and held on to him as he cried for his friend.

Luke gave them a few minutes together before he approached again. "If we leave now, we can make it back in time to see Alvin's school pageant."

Emma drew away from Roy and smoothed his jacket with her hands. "Will you be okay? Will you write? I'll be mad if you don't. I will send you money if you need it."

"Alvin's gonna be pretty upset with me if I miss his solo."

Luke smiled, knowing one innocent lamb was about to return to the fold. "He will. He's been practicing for weeks."

Roy rubbed his face on his sleeve. "You don't know the half of it. He sings in his sleep."

"If you want to ride along, that's fine with me, but I won't be able to bring you back here. I borrowed the car, and I have to return it."

Roy glanced around at the gray, dingy walls. "I reckon I'd rather spend Christmas at home than in this place."

The wail of a siren grew louder and then passed by. Luke looked at Roy. "Won't you miss all the lights and the excitement of the holidays?"

"The lights are mighty pretty, but I've noticed one thing about them."

"What's that?"

Luke looked up. "You can't see the stars at night because the light hides them. You may not be able to see them, but the stars are like God's love for us. Always there no matter what."

Emma laid a hand on Roy's shoulder. "Even when we aren't looking for it. His love is there. We'll wait while you pack."

A short five minutes later, he returned with a duffel bag over his shoulder. "I reckon I've got everything I need."

Emma had her brother back and she was grateful. All she needed now was to win Luke back. So where did she start?

Chapter Sixteen

Luke held his speed to just under the posted limit all the way back. It would be the last time he ever drove a car. To his surprise, he didn't mind the thought. A horse and buggy wouldn't carry him very fast, but it wouldn't carry him very far, either. From now on, he would be sticking close to home. He glanced in the rearview mirror. Close to Emma if she allowed it. He still wasn't sure how she felt about him.

Emma and Roy shared the backseat as Roy recounted his adventures. It was a healing time for them and Luke hated to see it end, but Zachariah's mailbox had come into view. Luke slowed and turned into the lane. As he pulled to a stop, the front door opened. Zachariah and Alvin stepped out onto the porch. No doubt they were wondering who was arriving in an English car.

When Roy and Emma got out of the backseat, Alvin gave a whoop of happiness and rushed toward them. Zachariah followed more slowly, but his grin was every bit as wide. Luke got out of the car and stood waiting for the reunion to end.

Emma, her face glistening with tears of joy, came to his side. "Come inside, Luke. I know Father will want to thank you for all you've done."

"I'd love to stay, but I have to get going. I need to return the car and make it to the school play on time. Hannah will never speak to me again if I'm late."

"We have to get ready as well. I reckon we'll see you there."

"I reckon."

As goodbyes went, it wasn't much. He wanted to get Emma alone and tell her that he loved her and that he couldn't live without her. But those words would have to wait for another day. "*Frehlicher Grischtdaag*, Emma."

"Merry Christmas to you, too, Luke." Her soft smile warmed his heart and gave him hope.

Emma and her family took their seats in the schoolroom that was quickly filling with family and friends of the children. Soon, all the lanterns in the room were turned down except one. Alvin walked out on the stage and into the circle of light, silhouetted against the backdrop painted to resemble the village of Bethlehem. After a hush fell over the room, Alvin's voice rang out pure and sweet, each note a living thing of splendor as he sang "While Shepherds Watched Their Flocks." Only the multitude of the heavenly hosts praising God on that first Christmas night could have sounded more beautiful. For the first time, she didn't see her brother—she saw a messenger of God bearing tidings of great joy. When his song was done, the shepherds entered the stage and the play began.

Tears filled Emma's eyes. She slipped her fingers into her father's hand, and he squeezed them gently. There were tears in his eyes, too. Emma listened, entranced by the age-old story and the peace that settled over her.

After one angel lost her wing and had to run back for it, the stage cleared again and Alvin walked to the center once more and began "The First Noel." No one moved. Even after the last clear note died away, a hush remained. It was as if no one wanted to mar the holiness filling the room.

Lillian walked to Alvin's side, touched his arm gently and turned to the audience. "That concludes our program tonight. There are refreshments at the back. Our scholars are so pleased that you could join us and we want to wish all of you a very Merry Christmas. *Frehlicher Grischtdaag.*"

Her father leaned over. "I think he will be the *Volsinger* one day."

"I think you are right." The *Volsinger* was the

man who began each hymn during the Amish church service. It was a solemn responsibility to lead the congregation in songs handed down through the generations.

The lights were turned up again, and the audience rose to enfold the excited children and move en masse toward the tables bearing goodies. Emma visited with her neighbors and friends, but she kept one eye on Luke where he stood with his family. Hannah was imploring her mother to fix her wing. As the crowd thinned out and began to go home, Emma made her way to her father's side. He sighed deeply and said, "Are you ready to go home?"

"You and the boys go on without me."

"Are you sure?"

"There's something I need to take care of, and you have a lot to discuss with your sons."

"I do. We'll see you later. *Guten nacht.*"

"Good night, *Daed.*"

As soon as her family went out, she fixed her gaze on Luke. What if she was wrong and he didn't feel the same about her? There was only one way to find out. He was getting his hat when she caught up with him. "It has been a remarkable night, thanks in large part to you, Luke."

He shook his head. "I didn't repeat a single poem or sing a note. The children made it special."

"I wasn't talking about the program."

His eyes searched her face. "I'm happy I was able to help."

She gathered her courage. "There is something else I'd like you to do for me tonight."

"Anything. What is it?"

"Would you walk me home?"

Luke's heart jumped into his throat. Had he heard her correctly? "I'm sure my family has room for you in the sleigh."

She looked down at her hands clasped in front of her. "It's not terribly cold. I thought a walk might be nice."

Happiness made him giddy. "It sounds *wunderbar*."

She looked up and met his gaze. "It does, doesn't it? It will only take me a minute to get my bonnet and coat."

Was she giving him another chance, or was this her way of saying a permanent goodbye? He closed his eyes and breathed a silent prayer, begging God for one more chance with the woman he loved. When he opened them, she was standing in front of him looking lovelier than ever.

"I'm ready."

That meant he had to be, too. *"Goot."*

They reached the road and he turned toward her home, but she stopped. "Would you mind if we went to the river?"

"I don't mind at all." She began walking, and he fell into step beside her.

A few straggling families from the school passed them. He politely turned aside several offers of a ride. Before long, the road was empty and they walked in silence. The crunch of snow under their feet was the only sound.

She looked up into the night sky. "How do the people in cities live without this beauty?"

"They have learned not to look. They pretend there is nothing above them." He wanted to hold her hand. Would she let him? He balled his fingers tight inside his coat pockets.

"How sad."

"It is a little, but people survive and thrive."

"The good Lord made us a resilient species."

"He did. Emma, can I ask you a question?"

"Certainly." She glanced at him shyly.

"Are you serious about Wayne?"

"Serious in what way?"

He stopped walking. "You know what I mean."

She hooked her arm through his. Astonished by the move, he let her pull him along. "I am no longer seriously considering Wayne as a suitor. Does that answer your question?"

"Is there anyone else?"

"*Ja,* there is."

His heart plunged to his boots. "Oh."

They reached the covered bridge and walked into the shadowy interior of the walkway. She shot him a sidelong glance. "Aren't you going to ask me who it is?"

He wasn't sure he wanted to know. So this was goodbye, then. "Whoever he is, he is a fortunate man."

"I'm glad you think so."

She stopped walking and turned to look out over the river. Luke leaned on the railing. Snow-covered trees lined the riverbanks. Overhead, the moon shone down, making it almost as bright as day. The dark water below them hissed and gurgled as it rushed around the pylons. Moonlight glinted in the ripples.

Emma looked at Luke. "Can I ask you a question?"

"Sure."

"Have you ever told a woman that you love her?"

"Never. I did tell a girl once when I was a foolish kid, but I didn't really know what those words meant. I've been wanting to say those words to one special woman. They burn in my heart."

"Why haven't you spoken of this?"

"Because I wasn't sure my feelings were returned. I couldn't imagine how they could be. The one I love deserves a much better man than I will ever be."

"You're not so bad. You have potential."

He grinned. "I do?"

"This woman you admire, she has faults, too. I'm sure of it."

"Only small ones."

"She not very humble. She is bossy and prideful."

"She is perfect because I only see her through the eyes of love. Don't tease me anymore, Emma. I love you with my whole heart and with my soul. I will love you forever if you give me the chance."

"That's a lot of love."

"Yes, it is." He pulled her into his arms. "Tell me that you love me, too."

Emma's heart swelled with joy. She had wanted to be in his arms for so long that it was hard to believe it was really happening. The words she had kept inside for years slipped effortlessly from her lips on a soft breath. "I love you, Luke Bowman. I always have. I always will."

"I don't deserve your love, Emma, but I will do everything within my power to be worthy of it until the day I die." He gently covered her lips with his own and Emma was swept away by the wonder of it.

Soft yet firm, the touch of his warm mouth against hers sent her mind reeling. The same wonderful feelings she remembered from her youth exploded in her chest, tempered by loss and honed by pain into an exquisite ache that made her press closer to him. All she wanted was to keep on kissing him. Her arms crept around his neck and he pulled her closer still.

He was the first to break away, drawing a deep unsteady breath that made her smile. He tucked her head beneath his chin. "I hate to be the practical one, but we should find somewhere warmer to continue this."

In the shadow of the covered bridge with the cold, bright moonlight sparkling on the icy waters below, Emma had never been warmer in her life. "I'm fine."

"I'm happy for you, but my toes are freezing."

She laughed. He could always make her laugh, and she loved that about him along with everything else, even his past. "Let's go to your house—it's closer."

He pulled her close again and kissed her. She didn't resist. When he drew back, he cupped her cheek with his hand. "I don't know why God chose to send us on such a roundabout journey to this moment."

"To make it that much sweeter for us. So that we'll never take our feelings for granted."

"That's what I think, too." He bent and kissed her again.

She threaded her fingers through his hair and kept him close when he would have pulled away. "Your toes will thaw. We might not find this much time alone together for ages."

"That is why I want you to marry me. I plan to spend a lot of time kissing you. Will you marry me, Emma?"

"Gladly. And I plan to spend a great deal of time kissing you back." She smiled and did just that.

Epilogue

❧

Alvin rushed into the kitchen. "I see them coming up the lane. They're almost here."

"Calm down." Emma smiled as she pulled on her coat. "You act as if you have never gone caroling before."

"I just want the people to like our songs and feel the happiness of the season."

Roy strolled into the room. "I remember the time you were so nervous to sing in front of people that you threw up on *Daed*'s shoes."

"I didn't."

"I believe that was you, Roy," Emma teased. She was secretly as excited as Alvin at the prospect of traveling to the community of Litchfield. Ten of the *kinder* from Alvin's school had been invited to sing at the nursing home there. Isaac Bowman was collecting some of the children and parents in his bobsled. They would meet up with the others at the retirement center and carol to various neighbors as they traveled home. And Luke would be with them. She couldn't imagine being happier.

Emma hustled her brothers outside. Her father waved to them from the door. His store was ready to open the next morning but he didn't want to leave it. Emma had seen him walking up and down the aisles, touching some of the items, straightening them and dusting others. He was as happy as he could be among his things displayed for everyone to see. She prayed he would enjoy his store for many years before the Lord called him home.

The gray draft horses and large sled stopped in front of the house. Isaac had outfitted his sled with wagon sides and filled the interior with benches. There were already a dozen people aboard. The men and boys in dark coats and black hats marked the riders as members of the Amish faith. The women and girls wore dark coats and black bonnets with bright quilts spread over their laps.

Emma put out her arms to stop the boys from rushing down the steps. "Remember that you have been invited to share the joy of this season with people who may not have families to care for them or who may be too ill to be in their own homes. No rowdy behavior."

"*Ja,* sister," they said in unison.

With that, she stepped aside and watched them

rush out. She settled her black traveling bonnet over her *kapp* and followed them. Luke was sitting in the driver's seat. Her pulse jumped a notch higher.

He tipped his hat to her. "My father has a head cold and has chosen to stay home. I hope you don't mind that I'm taking his place."

"Of course not." Spending an entire evening in Luke's company was exactly what she wanted to do. She climbed up and took a seat beside him.

Hannah leaned in between them. Her bright eyes sparkled as she clapped her hands together. "I have new mittens. See?"

Emma dutifully inspected them. "They are very nice mittens."

"*Onkel* Luke bought them for me for Christmas 'cause I lost my others."

Emma smiled at him. "That was very nice of your *onkel*. You must be extra careful with them."

"I will. Did you get something for Christmas?"

"I did. My brothers bought me material for a new dress. Isn't that funny? Who would think of boys shopping for dress material? My father gave me a new set of dishes. They aren't exactly new, but they are new to me. They have pretty pink flowers on them."

"I like pink flowers."

"You should sit down, Hannah," Luke said.

"The road is rough here and I don't want you to fall."

"Okay." She returned to her mother's side.

Emma shot him a sidelong glance. "The road is just as smooth here as anywhere else."

"I see that now, but I was sure it would be bumpy. Besides, I wanted you all to myself."

"I'd hardly think we can be alone with a sled full of people."

He leaned toward her. "Maybe not, but I can pretend when you're sitting beside me that we are the only two people in the world."

His soft whisper sent shivers down her spine. "I like that. I shall pretend the same." She inched a bit closer and settled in to enjoy the ride.

"God willing, we will ride many miles seated beside each other," he said with a wink.

"God willing we will have a daughter like Hannah to occasionally come between us."

"I think we will have boys. There are only sons in my family, after all. Eight sons, that's what I predict."

"Well, then, I shall predict eight girls to liven our lives."

Hannah popped up between them again. "*Mamm* says everyone can hear you."

Luke turned in his seat. "If everyone can hear me, I'd like to tell you that Emma has agreed to be my wife."

A cheer rose from his brothers. So much for

secrecy. She yanked on his coat to turn him back around, then she scooted to the end of the wagon seat, leaving plenty of room between them.

"We should warm up our voices before we get there," Alvin suggested, and the others agreed. He led them in the scales and then started "O Little Town of Bethlehem." Everyone joined in. The horses picked up the pace and their bells jingled merrily. Luke grinned at her, reached out and pulled her close.

She settled happily beside him.

"What song next?" someone asked.

Hannah spoke up. "Alvin, will you sing 'The First Noel'?"

As her brother's beautiful voice rang out across the fields, Emma whispered to Luke, "What was Christmas like in the *Englisch* world?"

"Light, parties, they sing the same song and other silly ones. A plump fellow with a white beard gets all the credit for the holiday. I think there are people who truly don't know the meaning of the day. They don't know that God sent us the greatest gift in His only Son."

"How sad. They need to experience an Amish Noel."

Hannah leaned in between them again. "If all the *Englisch* came with us, this sled would be very crowded."

Luke gently pushed her back with a hand on her head. "It already is."

Hannah giggled and Emma scooted over to make room for her. Lifting the child to the front seat, Emma endured Luke's scowl. She knew it was faked. "Christmas is about sharing our joy. There is no better messenger than a child to show us the way."

Hannah looked at her. "I wasn't the messenger. I was an angel."

Luke hugged her and winked at Emma. "How right you are. Merry Christmas."

* * * * *

Dear Reader,

I hope you are enjoying my new series, The Amish Bachelors, as much as I am enjoying discovering what makes the Bowman brothers tick. In all honesty, Luke was my biggest challenge to date. He's not a character that shares easily. I knew some of his history, but uncovering what made him tick was hard work. Helping him reunite with his former love was even harder. "Once burned, twice shy" was Emma's motto where Luke was concerned. Emma had to learn to trust, and Luke had to learn to accept forgiveness and rely on the Lord. That's hard for many people, especially those struggling with addiction.

I think I'm going to share Timothy's story next. In fact, I know I am. He clearly likes Teacher Lillian, but what is keeping her from returning his affections? I have an idea, but I will have to write the book and see what she reveals to me. Writing for me is always like Christmas shopping. I think I know what I want to get my friends or my family, but when I'm in the store, the perfect gift idea will pop into my head and I'm off to find it. I'm a last-minute shopper. Planning ahead takes the fun out of it for me. I plan my books, but my characters always pull me in a new direction.

I hope you are planning to have a joyous Christmas holiday. As you browse among the glittering lights and ornate decorations, take a minute to have an Amish Christmas Moment. An Amish Christmas Moment is taking a few seconds to close your eyes and give thanks for the gifts our Father has bestowed on you. To remember your family and your neighbors with kindness in your heart and strength in your soul. Life isn't easy. It wasn't meant to be, but moments of joy sprinkle all our lives with grace.

Merry Christmas to you and yours, and don't forget to take an Amish Christmas Moment at least once in your busy day.

Blessings,

Patricia Davids

YES! Please send me **The Montana Mavericks Collection** in Larger Print. This collection begins with 3 FREE books and 2 FREE gifts (gifts valued at approx. $20.00 retail) in the first shipment, along with the other first 4 books from the collection! If I do not cancel, I will receive 8 monthly shipments until I have the entire 51-book Montana Mavericks collection. I will receive 2 or 3 FREE books in each shipment and I will pay just $4.99 US/ $5.89 CDN for each of the other four books in each shipment, plus $2.99 for shipping and handling per shipment.*If I decide to keep the entire collection, I'll have paid for only 32 books, because 19 books are FREE! I understand that accepting the 3 free books and gifts places me under no obligation to buy anything. I can always return a shipment and cancel at any time. My free books and gifts are mine to keep no matter what I decide.

263 HCN 2404   463 HCN 2404

Name	(PLEASE PRINT)
Address	Apt. #
City	State/Prov.	Zip/Postal Code

Signature (if under 18, a parent or guardian must sign)

Mail to the **Reader Service:**
IN U.S.A.: P.O. Box 1867, Buffalo, NY 14240-1867
IN CANADA: P.O. Box 609, Fort Erie, Ontario L2A 5X3